GOOD-BYE, GARNET

Faster than The Saddle Club could believe, Veronica had Garnet tacked up and in the indoor ring. It was clear that the mare was as fresh and flighty as the day before. She danced at the end of the reins before Veronica quieted her long enough to get on, then shied and broke into a trot at once.

Standing with the Kingsleys at the edge of the ring, Carole said, "Boy, Garnet's behaving well today. She's usually much worse."

Henrietta sneered. "It's nothing a good crop and spurs won't fix," she said.

"Quite right, darling! Discipline is the key! You'll have her behaving in no time," Mrs. Kingsley bellowed.

THE SADDLE CLUB

STABLE FAREWELL

BONNIE BRYANT

A SKYLARK BOOK
NEW YORK • TORONTO • LONDON • SYDNEY • AUCKLAND

RL5, 009–012

STABLE FAREWELL
A Bantam Skylark Book / December 1995

Skylark Books is a registered trademark of Bantam Books,
a division of Bantam Doubleday Dell Publishing Group, Inc.
Registered in U.S. Patent and Trademark Office and elsewhere.

"The Saddle Club" is a registered trademark of Bonnie Bryant Hiller.
The Saddle club design/logo, which consists of
a riding crop and a riding hat, is a
trademark of Bantam Books.

"USPC" and "Pony Club" are registered trademarks of
The United States Pony Clubs, Inc., at The Kentucky Horse Park,
4071 Iron Works Pike, Lexington, KY 40511-8462.

ISBN 0-553-48267-X

Published simultaneously in the United States and Canada

Bantam Books are published by Bantam Books, a division of Bantam Doubleday Dell
Publishing Group, Inc. Its trademark, consisting of the words "Bantam Books" and
the portrayal of a rooster, is Registered in U.S. Patent and Trademark Office and in
other countries. Marca Registrada. Bantam Books, 1540 Broadway, New York,
New York 10036.

PRINTED IN THE UNITED STATES OF AMERICA

OPM   0 9 8 7 6

I would like to express my special thanks
to Caitlin Macy
for her help in the writing of this book.

CAROLE HANSON PAUSED in the driveway of Pine Hollow Stables. Her eyes swept over the picture-perfect scene— the neat barns and indoor ring, the fenced paddocks, and the rolling pastures beyond. Even in the middle of winter, with the bare trees and frozen puddles, it was probably her favorite place in the world. She breathed deeply to inhale the horsey smells and then ran for the barn.

One of the first things she noticed, once inside, was a large sign on the bulletin board outside Max Regnery's office. It said simply Horse for Sale—Ask Max. Carole stared at it in confusion. Max, the owner of Pine Hollow and its chief riding instructor, often let people post notices on the bulletin board about horses for sale, but usually they described the horses. Without knowing anything about a horse's size, breeding, and experience, you couldn't tell if it would be suitable. But Carole was too excited to wonder about the mysterious sign for long.

"We thought you'd never get here!" Stevie Lake exclaimed as she burst into the warm tack room.

"How long have you been here?" Carole asked, surprised.

"Oh, forever," Stevie said, her hazel eyes twinkling.

"In other words, about five minutes," Lisa Atwood commented dryly as she walked in behind Stevie.

Carole chuckled and gave her two best friends a spontaneous hug of greeting. They'd gotten back a few days earlier from a trip out West to the Bar None Ranch and had only managed one quick ride at Pine Hollow since then. Over the Christmas holidays, a snowstorm had stranded the girls at the Bar None. They always loved visiting Kate Devine at her parents' ranch, but none of them had planned to be away from home for Christmas, so they were still basking in the warm feeling of being back.

"Something must have happened to me out West," Stevie said solemnly. "I was actually glad to see my brothers again—even Chad!"

S T A B L E   F A R E W E L L

The girls laughed. Stevie's feuds with her three brothers, and especially Chad, were notorious.

"I was happy to go home, too, but somehow I didn't *really* feel I was home until I got to Pine Hollow," Carole said, looking around appreciatively at the rows of shining bridles and saddles.

Stevie and Lisa nodded knowingly. Of the three of them, Carole was probably the most horse-crazy. She thought about horses twenty-four hours a day and wanted to be a professional rider, a trainer, or maybe an equine veterinarian when she grew up.

"I agree: Pine Hollow is where The Saddle Club belongs," Lisa said. She was referring to the group that the three of them had started. The only requirements for membership were, one, being wild about horses and, two, being willing to help one another out in any situation. At Pine Hollow the girls took lessons, participated in Pony Club, helped with the chores, and held many spontaneous Saddle Club meetings. Stevie and Carole also boarded their horses, Belle and Starlight, at Pine Hollow. Lisa usually rode one of the school horses, a former racehorse named Prancer.

"So, Stevie," Carole queried, "if you've been here so long, I guess you've already said hi to Belle today, huh? You probably don't want to bother seeing her now, do you?"

Stevie grinned. Since she was constantly teasing people and playing practical jokes, she was used to getting a taste of her own medicine every so often. "Actually, Lisa and I were just on our way out when you came in." She linked arms with the other two and led them out the door.

All three of them had to stop themselves from sprinting to greet their horses. They knew they couldn't run inside the barn, though, so they walked as fast as they could down the aisle where the horses were stabled. On their way, they passed Max's bulletin board and Carole pointed out the strange sign. Lisa and Stevie agreed that it did seem short for an advertisement, but they soon forgot about it as they joined their horses.

When Carole had given Starlight a huge hug and fed him a couple of carrots, she took off his blanket and led the bay gelding out for a grooming. Stevie and Lisa followed suit with Belle and Prancer. They cross tied the horses close to one another so that the girls could talk. "I knew Max and Red would feed them, and turn them out, and clean their stalls but still . . . ," Carole began, pausing to tap her currycomb against her boot. Red O'Malley was Max's head stable hand and right-hand man around Pine Hollow.

"But still," Stevie continued, "nothing compares to the love we three lavish on them, does it?"

4

"My, aren't we sounding proud of ourselves today," a man's voice said. Stevie turned in alarm to see who had overheard her. She smiled when she saw that it was Max and that he was kidding.

Carole and Lisa looked up from their grooming to greet their instructor. "Hey! You weren't here to welcome us back the other day. Didn't you miss us, Max?" Stevie said, trying her best to look innocent but failing entirely. Although The Saddle Club pitched in a lot around Pine Hollow, they—and especially Stevie—were also known for stirring up trouble.

Max tactfully avoided answering the question. But he did seem as glad to see the girls as they were to see him. He asked all about their trip West and assured them that Starlight and Belle had spent lots of time outdoors in the paddock to make up for the exercise they had lost through not being ridden. "And Lisa, I only let a couple of the more advanced students ride Prancer, so none of your good work with her has been undone," he said.

They all thanked Max profusely until he cut them off with a wave of his hands. "Enough! I've got a lesson to teach, so consider yourselves welcomed back, all right?" The girls nodded eagerly.

When Max had gone, they went back to their grooming in earnest.

"You know, when we took our first ride after we got back from the Bar None, I was so excited to be with Starlight that I hardly noticed how clean he looked," Carole mused. "But now that I think about it, he looked as good as he always does."

"That's funny, because, come to think of it, Belle was really clean, too," said Stevie. She stepped back to look at the bay mare.

"Maybe it's because of their blankets," Lisa suggested. All three horses wore blankets in the winter when the temperature dropped below a certain point. Willow Creek, Virginia, where they lived, never got extremely cold, but for thin-coated Thoroughbreds like Prancer and Starlight and a half-Saddlebred–half-Arabian like Belle, the extra layer was an important source of warmth.

"The blankets help, but they don't keep their coats in such good condition," Carole said. "The only thing that does that is grooming. Regular grooming. And we've only groomed them once since we got back."

"Do you think Max groomed them while we were away?" Stevie asked.

Carole shook her head. "He wouldn't have had the time. I don't think he even grooms the horses he owns. That's all left to the riders."

"The riders and one other person," Lisa put in. "Red."

"Of course!" Stevie exclaimed. "How could we forget?" Not only did Red O'Malley always finish his assigned tasks, but he also constantly found ways to be even more helpful to Max and the Pine Hollow riders.

Leaving Lisa to keep an eye on their horses for a minute, Carole and Stevie went to track down the stable hand. They found him in Delilah's stall, teaching two of Max's beginning students how to braid a mane. As usual, he brushed off the girls' thanks. "It's easy to keep bays clean, anyway," he said.

"But Red, seriously, Starlight and Belle are glowing," Carole insisted.

"Yeah. They look every inch as good as they do when we're at home," Stevie said.

Red smiled. "It was my pleasure. You've helped me so many times in the past that I was glad of a chance to pay you back a little. Besides, I know how well you look after your horses. You really set an example around here that *everyone* should follow." With that, he turned back to Delilah and the braiding lesson.

Red's emphasis on the word "everyone" was not lost on Carole and Stevie. He hadn't come right out and said it, but they guessed that he was contrasting them—quite favorably—with Veronica diAngelo. Veronica was a vain, spoiled girl who often ignored her Arabian mare, Garnet.

7

She always expected Red to do her work for her. The situation was even more frustrating because grooming privately owned horses was not part of Red's job.

Lisa bristled when they repeated Red's comments to her. "Veronica is about as much help to Red as an early frost is to a farmer," she said. "But it's too early in the New Year to let her bother us. Let's just go for a long trail ride and forget all about it."

"Great idea," Stevie replied. "I'll bet Belle can't wait to get outside and stretch her legs. What do you say, Carole?"

"Um. Actually, I have other plans," said Carole, a blush spreading up her cheeks.

"Other plans? What other plans?" Stevie demanded.

Carole explained that when she had arrived home from the Bar None, there had been several phone messages from Cam Nelson. Cam was a boy she had met at last year's Briarwood Horse Show and whom she had seen every so often since then. The two of them shared a true, deep, and very serious commitment to horses, and even though Carole hadn't spent that much time with Cam, she certainly found him interesting. He was the closest thing to a boyfriend she had ever had.

"So what did he say?" prompted Stevie, who wasn't known for holding back when she wanted to find out something about someone's life.

8

"He called the first time a few days before Christmas to see if we could do something together over break. And then he called again when he expected me to be home, but we were stranded out West. He sent me a Christmas card, too," Carole added.

"Wow. You've sure been on his mind," Lisa said appreciatively.

Carole looked a little sheepish. "I guess I should admit that he's been on my mind, too. I sent him a postcard from the Bar None."

"You were thinking about Cam *and* Gary?" Stevie teased. Gary was a country-and-western singer Carole had met on their trip to the Bar None. She'd had a big crush on him until she realized that he was in love with someone else—himself.

"Let's just say I sent the card to Cam on the last day of our trip," Carole said, smiling. She had been thrilled when she got home and found Cam's card. It meant that he had been thinking about her when she had been thinking about him.

Lisa told Stevie to be quiet so that they could hear the rest, and Carole continued. "The end of the story is that when I called him back, we talked for nearly an hour, and today he's bringing Duffy to Pine Hollow to join me and Starlight on a trail ride." After a pause, she added, "I hope

9

you don't mind going without me, but . . ." Instead of finishing her sentence, she ended up grinning from ear to ear. For the first time, she had begun to think of Cam as a possible real boyfriend, and she couldn't hide how excited she felt.

"Mind going without you? Are you kidding? We're happy to go without you if it's because you're going with Cam," Stevie said.

Lisa gave Carole's arm a squeeze. "I hope you guys have a great ride," she said.

In a semidaze, Carole went back to Starlight to finish grooming him. She still had some time before Cam was due and she wanted to make her horse shine.

While Carole fussed over Starlight, Stevie and Lisa tacked up and cheerfully headed out together. They weren't the least bit offended that Carole wanted to ride with Cam alone. They even decided to change their normal route a little so that Cam and Carole could have a nice, private ride.

THE RIDE, CAROLE thought, was almost magical. From the moment she mounted Starlight and walked up beside Cam and Duffy, she felt as if she were in a dream. She found herself completely relaxed around Cam, and they immediately began to talk about horses. As they had before, the

10

two of them shared training techniques and bounced ideas off each other. Just when Carole was thinking how well Cam had Duffy going, Cam said he thought Carole and Starlight made a great pair.

"He's a little fresh today. He's only been ridden once since I got back," Carole said modestly. She had told Cam about the adventure at the Bar None that had kept her away.

"Maybe he just needs a good canter," Cam suggested.

That was all the invitation Carole needed. She urged Starlight into the faster gait. In a minute Cam did the same and the two horses, the bay and the chestnut, cantered along beside each other. "Hey! I think they like each other!" Cam called, pointing to the two sets of pricked ears.

Carole nodded, smiling back at him. She noted, not for the first time, what an excellent horseman Cam was. He sat tall and straight in the saddle, and he easily kept Duffy collected. What was even more impressive was that Cam had trained Duffy largely by himself in the years he had owned the gelding.

When they got to the woods, they slowed to a walk and went single file with Carole leading. Walking was as much fun as cantering for Carole because she and Cam could resume their conversation. Eventually they moved from

11

talking about horses to other subjects, and Carole was excited to find out that the two of them had other things in common. Some of them were silly, unimportant things—they both liked peanut butter cookies better than chocolate chip, and they both had gone to Disney World when they were eight—but they made Carole feel closer to Cam anyway. Every little fact that she learned about him made her like him more.

The woods were gray and brown, drab winter colors, but to Carole everything looked beautiful. When they finally turned for home, she found herself wondering when she would see Cam again. She wished the ride could continue forever, but all too soon they reached the Pine Hollow driveway. Cam dropped neatly to the ground, giving Duffy a good pat. Carole jumped off Starlight, too.

"I thought I'd give Duffy a drink before heading home," said Cam.

"Sounds good," Carole replied. After the two of them had rolled up their horses' stirrups and loosened their girths, she showed Cam to the outside watering trough, which Max kept heated in the winter.

"Boy, we were out a long time—nearly an hour and a half," Cam said, glancing at his watch.

"Really? It didn't seem long at all," Carole said.

"It sure didn't. I guess because we talked the whole way," Cam said.

"Yeah." For some reason, Carole felt suddenly shy. She couldn't think of what to say next. She started fiddling with her reins and patting Starlight. Then she noticed that Cam looked kind of awkward, too. He was tapping his crop against his boot.

"Well, I—"

"We could—"

The two of them looked at each other and laughed: Both of them had tried to break the silence at the same time.

"You go first," Carole said.

"Oh, no—ladies first," Cam insisted, smiling.

"Well, I was just going to say that I had a really good time," Carole said.

"Me too," said Cam. "And if it's okay with you, I'd like to call you again. Maybe we could do something else together soon."

Carole nodded, her eyes shining. "That would be great," she said.

Now that the air had been cleared, both of them relaxed and started talking again. They chatted easily while Cam walked Duffy back to the driveway and remounted. After a couple of minutes, Duffy began to fuss, tired of standing still with his rider on his back.

"I've got to teach him better manners," Cam said, shaking his head ruefully. "But for now, I guess we'd better get going, since it's a good four miles home. So I'll call you soon."

Carole watched as Cam turned Duffy and set off at a brisk walk. About halfway down the driveway he glanced back and waved. "Bye, Carole!" he called.

Carole put up a hand. "Bye, Cam!" She turned to Starlight. "Did you have a good time, too, boy?" she asked. In response Starlight, who was staring after his new friend, let out a long, shrill whinny.

Carole gave him a hug. "I'll take that as a yes," she said, laughing.

For the second time that day, Carole burst into the tack room, dying to see Stevie and Lisa. To her relief, they were inside soaping saddles. "Phew! I thought maybe you guys would have left already, and I wanted company while I cleaned my tack."

"Leave Pine Hollow before dinnertime on our second day back? Please!" Stevie said with mock disapproval. She paused, eyeing Carole curiously. "So, let's hear the details."

Carole was about to begin, but Lisa stopped her. "Stevie, is there anything you need to know that you can't tell from the look on Carole's face?" Lisa asked.

15

Stevie looked at Carole again, this time taking in her huge smile, her extrabright eyes, and her glowing cheeks. Then she smiled, too. "I'm glad you had a great date, Carole," Stevie said.

Although Carole admitted that Lisa was right—she was sure her happiness was written all over her face—she couldn't resist filling her friends in on a couple of details. "And you know what the best thing was?" she asked when she had finished.

"No, tell us," Lisa said.

"I really think Starlight and Duffy liked each other, too," Carole said.

Lisa and Stevie looked at each other and groaned good-naturedly. "Only you, Carole Hanson, would care if your horse got along with the guy's horse!" Stevie cried.

"Anyway, we're glad Starlight didn't try to bite Duffy or anything," Lisa said. "Now grab a sponge and we'll help you because we're almost done."

Carole obediently did as she was told, and before long she had placed her saddle and bridle alongside her friends' clean ones. For good measure, the girls soaped a couple of school saddles and tidied up the room a bit. When they were almost done, Meg Durham came in to put her tack away. Although Meg was about the same age as The Saddle Club girls, they didn't spend a lot of time with her. She was perfectly nice except for one thing: She was one of Veronica diAngelo's admirers. For some reason, a few of the girls who rode at Pine Hollow just couldn't seem to figure out that Veronica was about the worst person in the world to be friends with.

As soon as she saw them, Meg began chattering animatedly. "Hey, guys! Welcome back," she said. "Have you met Danny? What do you think of him? Isn't he gorgeous? Aren't we lucky to have such a beautiful boy come to Pine Hollow?"

Stevie, who had been trying to get a word in edgewise, piped up at once. "*What* beautiful boy? We didn't see any beautiful boys."

"Anyway, he couldn't top Cam," Carole whispered to Lisa.

"You haven't seen him yet?" Meg asked. "Boy, are you three ever in a fog."

"I'm not sure I'm so interested in seeing a beautiful *boy*," Stevie said. " 'Beautiful' isn't a very boyish adjective. How about 'cute'? I'd be more interested if he were cute."

"I'll remember to tell Phil that, Stevie," Lisa joked. Phil Marsten was Stevie's boyfriend. He lived in a neighboring town and belonged to Cross County Pony Club. Phil and one of his friends, A.J., were honorary members of The

17

Saddle Club. "I'll tell Phil you're interested in seeing cute boys, okay?" she added.

Before Stevie could respond, Meg continued. "Cute? He'd never be just cute with his breeding. And I doubt Veronica's family would want to pay that much money for a horse that sounded like a backyard pony. Honestly, 'cute'!"

The Saddle Club thought for a minute. Suddenly a few things were becoming clear. One of them was that Danny was not a boy—at least, not a human boy. "Are you saying that Danny is a horse?" Carole asked.

Meg gave her a funny look. "What did you think I was saying?"

"Never mind that," Stevie said. "The more important thing is that I thought I heard the name 'Veronica' a second ago."

"Of course you heard the name 'Veronica.' Danny is Veronica's Christmas present," Meg explained. "There was a picture of him under the tree for her Christmas morning. They trailered him over to Pine Hollow today."

"Christmas present? You mean she got a *horse* for Christmas?" Stevie demanded, incredulous. "What happened to argyle socks and leather gloves?"

"Obviously Veronica didn't need socks or gloves," Meg said, missing Stevie's joke entirely. "She has all that stuff."

"But she didn't need a horse, either," Lisa pointed out sensibly. "She has Garnet."

"Oh, this isn't just any horse," Meg said. "Danny is . . ." She paused to search for the perfect word. "Perfect, I guess you could say."

"Perfect?" The Saddle Club said in unison.

"Yeah, practically. He's an incredibly gorgeous Thoroughbred gelding, he has perfect manners, he's been schooled by some of the best trainers on the East Coast, he's hunted and evented and done dressage, *and* his show record is amazing. I've never seen such a wonderful horse. I mean—"

Before Meg could rave any more about Danny, Stevie cut her off. "All right. Let's go see this wonder horse," she said, her voice suspicious. For some reason, Stevie couldn't believe that the diAngelos could have found a horse as great as Meg was describing.

Meg, Stevie, Lisa, and Carole all piled out of the tack room to go and meet the new arrival. They didn't have to go far. A few people were gathered outside one of the stalls, oohing and aahing.

"But that's the mare-and-foal stall," Carole protested.

"Right. Since none of Max's mares is expecting this season, the diAngelos have rented out that stall for Danny.

19

They don't mind paying extra because they want him to be completely comfortable," Meg said.

Carole nodded but didn't say anything. She knew she wouldn't be able to reason with Meg, who was obviously quoting Veronica. But, as a good horsewoman, she thought it was stupid for people to lavish unneeded luxury on their horses. Danny would have been just as comfortable in a normal stall. It was clear that the diAngelos just wanted to make sure that everyone would notice their new purchase, and putting him in the double-sized mare-and-foal stall would draw more attention.

Together The Saddle Club peered into the stall at Danny. He was in the far corner finishing a flake of hay. Almost in unison, the three girls gasped. He looked like everything Meg had said and more, even just standing in his stall. He was an amazingly attractive horse. A tall, well-muscled dapple gray with a fine Thoroughbred head, he looked a little over sixteen hands high. He was perfectly filled out and conditioned. When he raised his head from the hay he gave his admirers a bored look out of his huge, dark eyes. Then he went back to eating.

"I don't know if I've ever seen such a great-looking horse," Lisa said in awe.

"His breeding must be fantastic," Carole breathed. "A horse like this can cost as much as a small house."

20

Stevie gritted her teeth and said nothing.

"It's funny, though, with Garnet . . ." Lisa let her voice trail off, remembering that they weren't alone. She didn't want to go on in front of Meg about Veronica's silly decision to get a new horse when she already had a perfectly good one. Meg would think they were just jealous.

Lisa could tell that Stevie and Carole were thinking the same thing, though. After all, it wasn't as if Veronica had physically outgrown Garnet, the way younger kids outgrew their ponies—as May Grover had with Luna. But Veronica also hadn't outgrown Garnet abilitywise: She wasn't so good that she needed a more challenging mount, as when Lisa had gone from riding Pepper to Delilah and then to Prancer. Garnet was still suited to Veronica's needs. The horse was pretty, well-behaved, and experienced, and, as far as they knew, Veronica wasn't interested in higher-level competition that might require a more athletic or spectacular horse. Of course, Veronica didn't always win at horse shows, but that was because she made mistakes, not because her horse was holding her back.

As The Saddle Club was considering all this, Veronica walked in. Seeing the appreciative crowd outside her horse's stall, she beamed. There was nothing Veronica liked better than being the center of attention, especially when it meant being able to show off.

21

Not wanting to listen to her bragging, Stevie turned and was attempting to slip away unnoticed when Veronica stopped her. "You don't have to rush off, Stevie. I don't mind if you want to look at my baby. He is a beautiful sight, isn't he?" she prompted.

Stevie nodded, her mouth set in a grim line. The most annoying thing about Veronica's conceited tone of voice was that this time nobody was going to be able to tell her that she was exaggerating. The horse *was* gorgeous.

"He's the most perfect show horse Daddy could find, and believe me, he searched long and hard. Here, boy, come say hello to Veronica." Veronica stuck out a manicured hand and waved it at Danny. Not surprisingly, the horse ignored her and kept munching. Stevie stifled a grin. Even the most perfect animal in the world knew better than to come when Veronica called.

Carole didn't want to encourage Veronica any more than Stevie, but she had to know about the horse's background. "Where did you find him?" she asked.

Veronica was only too eager to tell the story. "We bought him from a farm in Oakley, Maryland, that specializes in hunters and jumpers. Of course, you all probably wouldn't have heard of the place since it's kind of, well, out of your price ranges, but—"

"Oh, you mean Happy Vale Stables?" Carole asked non-

22

chalantly. Since she read every horse magazine there was, she knew all about the famous show stables.

Veronica gave her a condescending look. "My, my, so you have heard of it. Isn't that a surprise? Anyway, he's a purebred Thoroughbred with bloodlines that include Secretariat, and he belonged to the champion East Coast junior rider of the past two years. The only reason she sold him was that she needed a horse for the Olympics. And he already has points toward qualifying for the American Horse Show."

The Saddle Club was agog. Nobody said anything for a minute as they all tried to absorb the information. Secretariate, a son of Bold Ruler, was one of the most famous racehorses of all time. And the American Horse Show was the premier riding event in the country. They had gone to it once—to *watch*. It was almost unbelievable, but it sounded as if Veronica was implying that *she* intended to ride in it.

"Do you mean that you're going to take Danny in the show?" Carole asked, her eyes wide. It was something that she herself thought about only in her wildest dreams.

"Wouldn't you have to change your life completely? I mean, you'd have to go to all the major shows, all spring and all summer, and do really well if you want to qualify for the American," Lisa pointed out.

23

Veronica glared at them. "I'm perfectly aware of the qualification requirements for the show," she said icily. "And even if I don't do it this summer, I may later on. Who knows? Danny's only eight. And with a horse like him, anything is possible." She turned to Meg. "Did I tell you his show name yet?"

Meg shook her head. "No, but I'll bet it's good."

"It sure is since it really says it all: He's registered as Go For Blue."

Stevie snickered. "Gopher Blue? That's funny, I've never seen a blue gopher." She knew what Veronica had said, but she couldn't resist baiting her.

"Go For Blue as in 'go for a blue ribbon,' obviously," Veronica said with a sneer. "Anyway, Daddy really likes the name, too, because it was his idea that I get a proven champion. It's about time I had a really good horse to ride."

"But what about Garnet?" Lisa asked.

Veronica shrugged. "Garnet's a sweet horse, but I'm through with her."

"What do you mean, 'through'?" Carole demanded.

"I'm selling her. Didn't you see the sign by the office? It isn't that my parents couldn't afford to let me keep two horses, it's just that when you have a horse like Danny you really aren't interested in one like Garnet. Stevie, perhaps

24

you'll want to think about buying Garnet. She'd be a big step up from Belle. At least Garnet is a purebred." Veronica smiled sweetly and turned back to Meg.

Stevie was so mad she couldn't speak. It wasn't just that Veronica had a new, perfect horse and was casting off Garnet without a second thought. And it wasn't her insulting Belle, who was an American Saddlebred–Arabian cross. It was the stupidity of her comment: Everyone who knew anything about horses knew that some of the best horses for showing and eventing were mixed breeds. Half the Olympic team rode Thoroughbred or warmblood crosses, for heaven's sake! But to Veronica the brand name was everything—in clothes and in horses. To her "purebred" was a label that she could throw around to impress people.

Seeing Stevie's face grow red and her hands clench into fists, Carole and Lisa guided her away from Meg and Veronica. Veronica ignored them, leading Danny out to the cross-ties and cooing over him. "You're my perfect little horsey, aren't you, Danny-boy?" she murmured.

"Oh, *gag*," Stevie muttered.

As The Saddle Club walked down the aisle, they passed Garnet's stall. All three of them stopped to look at the mare. "Boy, Veronica really knows how to get a horse into condition for being sold, doesn't she?" Carole said sarcastically. In contrast to Danny, who had been groomed until

25

he was immaculate, Garnet was a picture of neglect. Her mane was long and unkempt, and she had a large manure stain on one of her hind legs. What was worse, her stable sheet had become so twisted that she was almost entangled in it. Shaking her head in disgust, Carole said she would fix the blanket.

"I wouldn't bother if I were you," Stevie said, almost sputtering. "Veronica doesn't deserve our help."

Lisa and Carole exchanged glances. Clearly Stevie was so angry that she didn't know what she was saying.

"Veronica doesn't deserve our help, but her horse does," Carole said quietly.

Almost at once Stevie realized how harsh her own words had sounded. "You're right, Carole—I just can't put up with Veronica any longer!"

"So let's focus on Garnet," Carole said. She entered the mare's stall to check the horse over more carefully. First she gave Garnet a good pat, noticing that she seemed edgier than usual. The stall's bedding was dug into ruts from her constant pacing, a clear sign of boredom. As Carole carefully unhooked the sheet, straightened it, and rebuckled the straps, she scratched Garnet's back and spoke to her soothingly. "You're probably bored out of your mind, aren't you? I would be, too, cooped up in this stall . . . I wonder how long it's been since anyone paid attention to you." Carole knew that with their busy schedules, Red and Max could hardly be expected to exercise Garnet. No doubt they had mentioned the horse's boredom to Veronica, who had probably laughed it off.

It made Carole's blood boil to see a nice, well-behaved horse like Garnet left to rot in her stall. "Maybe Garnet's getting sold will end up being a good thing: Somebody who deserves her might buy her," she mused aloud.

"But who on earth would buy a horse who looks like Garnet does?" Stevie asked.

"Yeah, she looks like nobody cares about her," said Lisa.

Carole frowned thoughtfully. "She may look like that, but it's not true."

"What do you mean?" Stevie asked.

"I mean, somebody *does* care about Garnet," Carole said. "Three somebodies, in fact, and you know who I mean."

"Us?" said Lisa, catching on.

"Us," Carole said firmly.

3

ON THE FOLLOWING Tuesday afternoon, the girls had their usual group lesson. Or at least Stevie, Lisa, and Carole were *expecting* the usual lesson. What they got instead was a "Veronica and Danny" exhibition. From the moment Max called the group to order to the moment he told them to dismount, Veronica and Danny could do no wrong.

Watching them trot and canter perfect circles and figure eights, halt on command, leg-yield down the long side of the ring, and lengthen and shorten stride at the trot, Lisa drew even with Carole and Stevie and whispered, "They're perfect, aren't they? Really and truly perfect."

"You mean *Danny's* perfect," Stevie corrected her. "All Veronica has to do is sit there and look pretty. Danny's the total push-button horse."

"Push-button?" Lisa repeated.

Stevie nodded. "It's just what it sounds like: a horse that behaves like a machine. You push the buttons and it performs perfectly."

Carole looked around cautiously before responding. Normally Max would have yelled at the three of them the minute they started talking, but today even he was caught up in watching the new arrival. "I have to agree," Carole said, glancing at Danny as he made another perfect transition, "and a push-button horse is exactly the kind of horse Veronica should be riding. As we all know, she doesn't want to take the time to get involved with actually training a horse."

After about forty minutes of flat work, Max set up a few simple fences to end the lesson with some jumping. If anything, Danny was even more unbelievable over fences. Veronica hardly moved in the saddle, but they took each jump from the exact right spot and sailed over in a perfect arc. Danny snapped his knees up athletically and settled right down upon landing. It was obvious that the two-foot, six-inch schooling jumps were child's play for such a great jumper. After every fence, Veronica gave Danny a huge pat and acted as if he had just cleared a six-foot oxer.

Mercifully, Max called the lesson to a halt the minute the hour was up, reminding them to walk their horses on a lead until they were cool. Stevie, Lisa, and Carole walked beside one another, as usual, so that they could talk, but surprisingly enough, nobody had anything to say. Danny's perfection seemed to have put a damper on everything. Even though they knew that Carole was right and that it was better to ride horses that needed some training—and in the long run they would be better riders because of that —it was frustrating to see Veronica get perfect results without doing anything. All of them, at some point or another, had wished they had a push-button horse. Now Veronica had one.

"Good boy, Danny. You were as good as I knew you'd be. You're worth every cent Daddy paid for you!" The Saddle Club turned in unison to watch Veronica go by. For the first time they could remember, she was actually walking her own horse to cool him off. Obviously—and completely typical of Veronica—she thought Danny was more deserving than Garnet because Danny had cost more.

"By the way, Veronica, how's *Garnet* doing these days?" Carole asked, unable to keep the sharp edge out of her voice.

Veronica stopped Danny and turned around. "Garnet? I hadn't really noticed. I'm sure she's fine. In case you've forgotten, Carole, it's Red's job to take care of the horses," she added sweetly.

Ignoring her, Carole persisted. "She looked a little bored the last time I saw her. She was pacing in her stall."

Veronica shrugged. "Too bad for Garnet. Right now Danny has all of my attention, as I'm sure you can understand."

Before Carole could retort, Max appeared at the door to the indoor ring. "Veronica, don't forget that a prospective buyer is coming to look at Garnet in a few minutes. You'd better hurry up with Danny and get her ready. And be prepared to show Garnet to them. It won't take more than an hour."

"An hour!" Veronica wailed. "But Max, that's impossible. Mother's picking me up in five minutes to go shopping!"

"Well, it's your horse, and you're trying to sell her," Max said evenly.

"Can't you get Red to do it?" Veronica whined.

While Max explained that Red had far too much to do to show Garnet to buyers, Carole had a quick conference with Stevie and Lisa. Carole had always been interested in knowing more about selling horses in case she became a

31

dealer when she grew up, but mostly she was concerned about Garnet. Stevie and Lisa were happy to help. "I've been worried about Garnet, too," Lisa said. "She's such a sweet mare, and besides, no horse should be ignored the way I'll bet Garnet has been."

Carole interrupted Max and Veronica to volunteer for the job. Max looked relieved, Veronica looked surprised, but both were happy to let The Saddle Club take over. Stevie, Lisa, and Carole agreed to meet at Garnet's stall as soon as they had put Belle, Prancer, and Starlight away. As they were untacking they saw Veronica giving Danny horse treats and fussing over him before she left.

"Will wonders never cease?" Stevie muttered. Usually Veronica threw her reins at Red and hopped into her waiting car without so much as a pat for her horse.

"Yeah, next thing you know, she'll want to muck out Danny's stall, too!" Lisa replied.

"It's funny, though," Carole said, observing Veronica's lovey-doveyness toward her new horse, "Danny doesn't seem to respond the way Starlight, Belle, Prancer, or Garnet would. He's kind of standoffish toward Veronica."

Stevie and Lisa followed Carole's glance. The scene was almost comical: Even though Veronica was patting and praising Danny profusely, he was staring into the distance with a vacant expression in his eyes. He seemed to be

32

ignoring Veronica, the way he would ignore a fly that was
pestering him. With a final hug, Veronica turned to go. On
her way out the door, she turned and blew Danny a kiss,
but the gray head had already disappeared inside his stall.

"Maybe he's even more perfect for Veronica than we
realized," Lisa joked. "A *horse* that's as snobby as she is!"

Carole and Stevie laughed. They didn't have time to
ponder Danny's personality any longer, though. Just as
they finished putting their horses away, a girl in jodhpurs
and boots showed up with her parents in tow. Guessing at
once that she had to be the prospective buyer, the girls
went to introduce themselves. They were eager to give the
family a good first impression of Pine Hollow.

"You must be here to see Garnet," Stevie said. When
the girl nodded, Stevie introduced everyone. The girl's
name was Katie Miller. She was a tall, skinny eleven-year-
old, and she was looking for her first horse. She had heard
about Garnet through a friend of hers who took lessons at
Pine Hollow.

One look at one another and The Saddle Club knew
that they had all taken an instant liking to Katie. She was
bright, cheerful, and considerate. As they walked her
through the barn, she asked them a million questions
about Garnet—her likes and dislikes, her personality, her
talents.

Then The Saddle Club questioned Katie about her experience. Katie had been riding for several years. She did a little eventing and loved trail rides. "I want to try endurance riding, and I read that Arabians were great for it, so that was another reason I wanted to look at Garnet," she explained.

Leaving Carole and Stevie to talk with Katie, Lisa dropped back and began a conversation with Katie's parents. She had noticed that they looked kind of nervous and decided she would speak with them. She was usually pretty good at handling parents. Searching for a topic, she asked Mr. and Mrs. Miller if either of them rode.

The two adults shook their heads vigorously. "Oh, no. Neither Mr. Miller nor I have ever sat on a horse. We're dog people, raise Irish setters. We haven't the faintest idea where Katie got her love for riding." At this point Mrs. Miller paused to gaze fondly at her daughter, who was still talking a mile a minute. "But we're happy that she's so dedicated, aren't we, dear? And after four years of watching her improve, we've decided that she really deserves a horse of her own."

Mr. Miller nodded. "Right. And we want to find her a good horse," he said firmly.

"You mean a purebred Arabian like Garnet?" Lisa asked, testing them a little.

"Purebred, crossbred, rye bread—we wouldn't know the difference," Mr. Miller joked. "No, what we're interested in is a nice, safe horse for Katie. One that she'll feel comfortable on."

Lisa smiled at the man's answer. She didn't want to jump to conclusions, but it sounded as if Garnet was the perfect match for Katie and her parents. *Now if only they would like the mare and not notice that*— Lisa's thoughts were interrupted as the group reached Garnet's stall. Out of the corner of her eye, she saw Carole's and Stevie's dismayed looks before the girls pasted smiles on their faces. One look at Garnet and Lisa knew what was worrying them: The horse had never looked so bad. Her mane and tail were still tangled and unkempt, her sheet was twisted again, and to make matters worse, she was chewing impatiently on her stall door.

"What's she doing that for, Katie?" Mrs. Miller asked anxiously.

A little embarrassed, Katie explained that sometimes horses chewed wood out of boredom. "In winter horses stay inside more and they can get restless," she added.

The Saddle Club was glad to hear such a sensible answer from Katie. Still, they all felt bad. If they had been in Katie's place, they would've been a little worried, too. A horse that looked uncared for usually acted it as well. As quickly as they could, the three of them put Garnet on the cross-ties and began grooming her, trying to ignore Mr. and Mrs. Miller's comments about her condition. Even non-horse people could tell when an animal hadn't been looked after properly.

"Isn't she moving around a lot?" Mr. Miller asked, watching Garnet dance away from Carole. Carole had gotten the saddle and was attempting to put it on the mare's back.

"Yeah, Dad, she's got a lot of energy," Katie said. "Here, let me help." Katie went to Garnet's shoulder and stroked her and talked quietly to her. She didn't seem put off by Garnet's high-strung behavior. *At least not yet,* Carole thought, sliding the saddle into place.

"Now wouldn't you think someone would clip her whiskers?" Mrs. Miller remarked. "We always keep the dogs' nice and neat, even when we're not showing them." Carole looked at Lisa, who looked at Stevie, who grimaced. Mrs. Miller was right, of course. Even cleaned up a little, Garnet didn't look very good. With the long mane and whiskers she had a shabby appearance, and the manure stains on her hocks wouldn't brush out.

"Now, Mom, you always tell me that conformation is more important than a fancy trim job," Katie chided her mother.

To change the subject, Stevie broke in. "All right, looks like we're ready. Let's go to the indoor ring so you can see her in action," she said brightly.

Looking doubtful, Mr. and Mrs. Miller followed the girls to the ring. While Lisa got them settled in the small spectator booth, Stevie took Katie into the middle to watch, and Carole got Garnet ready to strut her stuff. First she made the mare stand so that Katie could take a look at her from all directions. Then she tightened the girth and prepared to mount. The whole time, she whispered earnestly to Garnet. "Behave yourself if you know what's good for you, okay? This is your chance to get a really great owner. You'll go on trail rides, you'll get lots of attention, and you'll never have to see Veronica diAngelo again. Got it?"

Unfortunately, although Garnet swiveled her chestnut ears back and forth and seemed to be paying attention, Carole knew the minute she got on that she was in for a difficult ride. The mare was full of pent-up energy from her long inactivity and kept trying to break stride, first from a walk to a trot, then from a trot to a canter. Carole sat tight and prayed that the Millers wouldn't notice.

Watching from the ground, Stevie and Lisa could tell that Carole was doing everything she could to mask and make light of Garnet's behavior. When Garnet shied violently, Carole pretended that she had asked for a canter.

When her canter got fast, Carole rose in her stirrups and acted as if she wanted to hand gallop. She put the mare through her paces several times, finishing up with a number of small jumps.

"Isn't she taking kind of a long time?" Lisa asked Stevie when Katie went to consult with her parents.

Stevie nodded. "The longer Carole rides her, the better chance there is that Garnet will settle down and behave for Katie," she whispered.

Finally Carole rode into the center of the ring to let Katie get on. As Stevie had predicted, Carole had worked out most of Garnet's high jinks. For longer than they expected, Garnet trotted along calmly, obediently responding to Katie's aids. Katie had the makings of a very good rider. She had the basics down, and she also really seemed to be enjoying Garnet. After fifteen minutes or so, she asked The Saddle Club to set up a few cross rails for her to try.

"Are you sure you want to jump, dear?" Mrs. Miller called.

"Yes, Mom! How else am I supposed to know if I like jumping her?" Katie called back.

Lisa, Stevie, and Carole had the jumps set up in a jiffy, and Katie made her first approach at a trot. Several strides away from the jump, Garnet broke into a canter and tried to rush the fence. Katie sat up and brought her back to a trot, circled, and reapproached.

"Be careful, dear!" Mrs. Miller cried.

Once again Garnet tried to bolt. This time Katie halted her. "Will you drop it to a pole on the ground?" she asked.

Impressed with Katie's knowledge, Carole lowered the two rails to the ground. Soon Katie had Garnet calmly trotting back and forth over them. Before dismounting she tried another cross rail, and Garnet went over it calmly. The Saddle Club breathed a collective sigh of relief. Garnet had acted up, and Katie had settled her without being too harsh. They were a good pair.

"So what do you think?" Lisa asked. The three of them had cooled Garnet off while Katie talked with her parents. Now they were waiting in the tack room for the news.

"If anyone could have sold her, it's you, Carole. That was some performance," Stevie said.

"The thing is, Katie and Garnet are perfect for each other. If only the Millers would realize that," Carole said. "Today was the worst day she's had in a long time, and Katie handled her fine."

"Shhh, here they come," said Lisa, putting a finger to her lips.

The girls stopped talking and listened. Through the

open door they heard Mr. Miller's voice. Then Katie said, "She's *not* a dangerous horse, Dad. She was just feeling her oats today. Can't we please, please get her?"

Mrs. Miller spoke up. "Honey, you have to remember that Garnet is the first horse we've looked at. It would be silly to buy a horse without comparing her to anything else, and we have several others to look at."

"But—," Katie started to say.

"Listen, we're not saying no, but we're definitely not saying yes, Katherine. That horse was acting up," Mr. Miller said.

The Saddle Club pretended to be busy as Katie and her parents came through the door. Katie looked crushed.

"We wanted to thank you girls for all your time," Mrs. Miller said, shaking hands with each of them.

"Yes, and we'll be in touch with you shortly," Mr. Miller said. "Now we'd better get going—almost suppertime for the dogs."

Katie stared glumly at the floor. On her way out, she turned and whispered, "It might still work out. Oh, I hope so!"

When she was gone, The Saddle Club sat down disappointedly. "Silly Garnet. If only she'd known not to act up, today of all days," Carole said.

"What can you expect after not being exercised for who knows how long?" said Stevie.

After a pause, Lisa said, "Hey, why are we getting upset already? Katie was great, but I'm sure there are other people like her."

Consoling themselves with the thought that another equally good buyer was sure to come along soon, the girls headed home. On their way out, they passed Garnet's stall. She poked her head over the door in a friendly manner, ears pricked, nose out. Carole and Lisa patted her, but Stevie shook her head at the mare. "Save it for the next buyer, honey," she said.

4

WHEN CAROLE GOT home she couldn't wait to share the day's events with her father. After her mother died, several years before, Carole had become particularly close to Colonel Hanson. She kept him filled in on all aspects of her life, especially Pine Hollow.

At dinner (turkey tetrazzini) and dessert (tapioca pudding), Carole chatted enthusiastically about Veronica, Katie, and the Millers until she noticed the amused expression on her father's face. "What's so funny, Dad?" she demanded.

Colonel Hanson smiled. "Nothing, honey," he said.

42

"Nothing, that is, except for the fact that every day since you got home, you've asked me if there were any messages for you."

Carole put her fork down. "Yes. And?"

"And today you didn't ask me," Colonel Hanson said. "That's all."

Carole raised her eyebrows at her father, but his poker face revealed nothing. "Dad, are you, by any chance, implying that today there *were* some messages?" she asked.

"Well, now, let me try to remember. Hmm . . . oh, yes, the cleaning lady called—"

"Dad."

"And I think somebody called about changing my racquetball game to Wednesday. And, let's see—"

"Dad!"

"Now, was there anything else? I can't quite—"

"*Dad!*" Carole fairly screamed.

Colonel Hanson grinned. "You got a message, too, honey. From one Cameron Nelson residing at Fifteen Strawberry Hill Lane." He paused to pull a scrap of paper out of his pocket. "The number is—"

At that Carole jumped up, grabbed the paper out of her father's hand, and fled from the table. She was halfway to her bedroom before she stopped and called back, "How do you know where he lives, anyway?"

"We had a conversation during the course of which I asked the young man's address," Colonel Hanson replied with mock formality.

Carole groaned inwardly. The idea of her father talking —about anything—with Cam was her worst nightmare. Still, it was great news that Cam had called her again so soon. Quickly she dialed his number. While she listened to the phone ringing, she suddenly felt nervous. Then she reminded herself that she was calling Cam, a very nice person who was her friend.

"Hello?"

"Ah—hello," Carole said finally, startled that a woman, who was probably Cam's mother, had answered. At least she sounded friendly. "Is Cam at home?"

"No, I'm sorry, he's not. He's gone to watch his brother's basketball game, and he'll be gone all evening," the woman said.

Carole felt her face fall. "Oh, I see."

"Could I give him a message?"

"Yes—ah, yes, please. Is this Mrs. Nelson?"

"That's right."

Carole thought for a split second, but she couldn't think of anything original to say. "Could you just tell him that Carole called?"

"Sure, Carole. I'll tell him," Mrs. Nelson said.

44

"Okay, thanks. Thanks a lot."

"You're welcome, dear. Bye-bye now."

"Bye." Carole waited until she heard the dial tone. Then she slowly hung up the phone and went to start her homework. She got out her math textbook and sharpened a pencil. Half an hour later she was still staring into space and doodling "Cam and Carole" on her notebook.

THE NEXT DAY The Saddle Club met at Pine Hollow after school. "Isn't that the diAngelos' chauffeur?" Lisa asked, watching a uniformed man get into a long sedan and drive off.

Carole nodded. "It sure is. I wonder what she's doing here today." Usually Veronica only showed up for lessons and Pony Club. She hardly ever came on a regular weekday afternoon.

"She's probably showing Danny off for some of her fans," Stevie guessed.

What they saw inside the stable was even more surprising. Not only was Veronica there, but she was grooming her own horse. She had Danny out on the cross-ties, and she was fussing over him as they'd never seen her fuss over a horse before. She had him brushed, with his mane and tail combed, and was busy painting polish on his hooves. Stevie, Lisa, and Carole stared in amazement.

45

"He's hard to take your eyes off, isn't he?" Veronica asked, standing up after the last hoof.

The three of them nodded blankly. Carole was the first to find her voice. "Don't you want to know how things went with Katie Miller yesterday?" she asked.

Veronica shrugged. "Sure, why don't you tell me?" she said.

Carole took a deep breath to keep herself from yelling at Veronica. Trying to make herself sound calm, she explained, "Actually, Katie really liked Garnet, and she'd be a great owner for her. She's a good rider and she wants to do a lot of trail riding. But Garnet was so keyed up, since she hadn't been ridden for so long, that Katie's parents didn't think she'd be safe for their daughter, so they're going to think about it for a while and look at some other horses."

"And it didn't help that Garnet looked like a complete mess," Lisa added dryly.

Veronica surveyed Danny's gray coat and rubbed at an imaginary spot with a cotton cloth. Finally she turned to The Saddle Club. "Is that all?"

Once again the girls nodded, speechless.

Veronica smiled. "Good, because it doesn't matter if that Katie whatever-her-name-was didn't want Garnet. The absolute perfect buyer is coming this afternoon—any minute now. Her name is Henrietta Kingsley. You've heard of the Kingsleys, haven't you?" she asked.

Stevie and Carole shook their heads, but Lisa nodded. Her mother made it her business to keep tabs on a lot of "social" people. "The Kingsleys are big financial powers in Washington, D.C.," she explained.

"Correct," Veronica said. "Daddy does business with them all the time, and when he told them about my pure-bred mare being for sale . . . well, it sounded like the perfect match for Henrietta. She's only been riding for six weeks, but Mother says she's really quite accomplished."

"Six weeks?" Lisa repeated. She was amazed that anyone would buy a horse after so short a time. She knew that six weeks after *she* had started riding, she certainly hadn't been ready to own a horse. She wasn't even sure she was ready to own one now. Before she could say anything more to Veronica, a car's wheels crunched on the gravel outside.

"That must be Henrietta!" Veronica squealed. She put Danny away and ran out to greet the Kingsleys. Carole, Lisa, and Stevie followed at a safe distance, curious to see the great Henrietta who was ready for her own horse after six weeks.

A huge, shiny Rolls-Royce had pulled up in the driveway. It was even bigger and shinier than Veronica's chauffeur-driven car. The Kingsleys' chauffeur—who was even taller and grander than Veronica's chauffeur— emerged from the driver's seat to help his passengers out. Henrietta and her mother got out, and both of them screeched and rushed toward Veronica, exchanging air kisses.

The Kingsley women were a commanding presence. They were tall, they were large, and they were loud. Mrs. Kingsley was wearing a full-length fur coat; a fur hat; a pair of long, black gloves; and high-heeled boots. But Henrietta was the real spectacle. The Saddle Club was used to Veronica's high-priced riding gear, but Henrietta obviously took everything a step further. She looked totally inappropriate for an everyday ride, in white breeches, a yellow vest, patent-leather-topped hunting boots, a stock tie, and, unbelievably, a shadbelly coat like the ones worn by Grand Prix dressage riders.

"Isn't that, like, *illegal?*" Lisa whispered, gaping.

Carole and Stevie giggled. "Not exactly illegal," Carole said. "But it's one of the grossest displays of money and ignorance that I've ever seen."

"We'll see how 'accomplished' she is," Stevie said darkly.

"Anyway," Mrs. Kingsley was saying—or rather, *yelling,* which, as Carole pointed out, was a more accurate word— "we want only the best for Henrietta. She's quite taken with riding, and Mr. Kingsley and I believe she has natural talent. You should see the way horses just love my daughter from the moment they see her. It's really quite beautiful."

"Oh, I'm *sure* it is," Veronica said with a sickening smile. "I've heard what a great rider she is after only six weeks."

"Daddy said I could get two or three horses if I want. Didn't he, Mother?" Henrietta demanded.

"Of course, dear, whatever you want, you shall have," said Mrs. Kingsley.

"Boy, Henrietta, you're sure lucky to have such nice parents," Veronica said.

The Saddle Club looked at one another in disgust. "I think I'm going to be sick," Stevie muttered. If there was anything more nauseating than Veronica being her normal self, it was Veronica kissing up to people who were richer and more important than she was.

"You can't be," Carole said sternly, "or you won't be able to watch Henrietta try to ride."

"Do you think she'll even want to get on once she sees Garnet?" Lisa asked, following the group inside.

When they reached Garnet's stall, Stevie went up to Veronica and gave her a wide-eyed look of amazement. "Wow, Veronica, I've never seen Garnet looking so nice!" she said in wonder.

Carole and Lisa practically fell over backward. Despite

49

having been groomed the day before, Garnet still looked scraggly. With all the time she had spent fussing over Danny, Veronica still hadn't managed to brush her, trim her whiskers, or pull her mane. After a second's thought—and a glance at Stevie's mischievous grin—Carole and Lisa caught on: Stevie was trying to scare the Kingsleys off. Immediately they joined in.

"She *does* look good," Carole said. "Not bad for a horse who's so second-rate compared to Danny."

Lisa pretended to admire Garnet and then asked, as if she had just noticed it, "Hey, you guys, look at the chewed wood on her stall. Isn't that a sign of cribbing?"

"Yes, it is," Carole replied. "And cribbing can be so dangerous. It can cause colic and all kinds of problems."

"Well, you know what they say: One vice leads to another. It looks like Garnet's been pacing in her stall. Look at that rut in the front," Stevie added cheerfully.

Unfortunately, the Kingsleys seemed more confused than alarmed by what the girls were saying. Veronica gave the three of them a dirty look and said loudly, "Mrs. Kingsley, Henrietta, I know you're interested in breeding, and I wanted to let you know that Garnet's bloodlines can be traced back eight generations without missing a horse, in a straight line to horses owned by the sultans of Arabia."

"That's just what we wanted to hear," Mrs. Kingsley

announced. "Now hurry up and put that saddle on so we can see her in action, will you?"

FASTER THAN THE Saddle Club could believe, Veronica had Garnet tacked up and in the indoor ring. It was clear that the mare was as fresh and flighty as the day before. She danced at the end of the reins before Veronica quieted her long enough to get on, then shied and broke into a trot at once.

Standing with the Kingsleys at the edge of the ring, Carole tried again. "Boy, Garnet's behaving well today. She's usually much worse."

Henrietta sneered. "It's nothing a good crop and spurs won't fix," she said.

"Quite right, darling! Discipline is the key! You'll have her behaving in no time," Mrs. Kingsley bellowed.

"What? Did someone say something?" Veronica called. She was cantering haphazardly around the ring.

The Kingsleys ignored her. Henrietta turned to Stevie, Lisa, and Carole. "Look, I don't want to tell your boss that you're slouching on the job, so why don't you make yourselves useful and give these boots a shine?" Henrietta stuck out a foot to be polished.

"We're not—" Carole started to protest, but Stevie elbowed her.

"This is too good to miss," she whispered. She whipped a towel out of her back pocket, knelt down, and spit all over Henrietta's boots. "Spit and polish still make the best shine," Stevie murmured. Lisa's hand flew up to her mouth as she stifled a giggle.

Eventually Veronica rode over to speak to the Kingsleys. She was panting and red in the face from trying to control Garnet. "All right, Henrietta. I've got her nice and warmed up, so why don't I give you a leg up?"

"I can hardly wait," Stevie whispered wickedly.

Henrietta looked up from consulting with her mother. "Oh, that won't be necessary. I've decided that I don't need to ride Garnet myself. Just have those copies of the bloodlines sent over in the morning, all right?"

"S-sure, I mean, of course I will," Veronica answered, taken aback.

"All right. So I guess she's mine, right, Mother?"

Mrs. Kingsley huffed and puffed a bit. "Now, don't get overexcited, dear. We can't consider the animal yours until she's got a definite seal of approval from Grandmama's veterinarian." The older woman turned to The Saddle Club. "I'll have the man flown up from the racing stable in Kentucky as soon as possible. If the horse passes inspection, we'll take her. Otherwise, no deal."

Stevie, Lisa, and Carole gaped at the Kingsleys. The vet

check was totally reasonable, of course. But never, in all of their years of riding, had they ever heard of anyone buying a horse without trying it. It was stupid, it was insane—and it was just the kind of thing you'd expect from Veronica diAngelo's "perfect buyers."

"But I LIKED the part when the man saved her from drowning," Carole protested. It was Friday night and she and her father were just coming home from seeing an Alfred Hitchcock movie called *Vertigo*.

"I guess you're just a sucker for the romantic touch," Colonel Hanson kidded.

Carole tried to give him a withering look but ruined it by running to the answering machine to check for messages. She still hadn't succeeded in actually talking to Cam. He had called when she was out and vice versa. Sure enough, there was a message tonight. Carole turned the volume up as soon as she heard Cam's voice. Was it her imagination or did he sound kind of upset?

"Hi, Carole, it's Cam calling," the message said. "Listen, I really need to see you—to talk to you—so I hope we'll catch up with each other soon. I'll keep trying. . . . I guess that's all. Okay, bye."

Carole played the message again to make sure she hadn't missed anything. Cam definitely sounded strange—upset or worried, maybe. It could be that he was just disappointed that they couldn't seem to connect. The annoying thing was that it was too late to call back now. Puzzling over the tone of the message, Carole brushed her teeth and got ready for bed. She drifted off to sleep thinking sweet thoughts about Cam.

THE NEXT MORNING Carole was almost late for the un-mounted Horse Wise meeting at Pine Hollow. Horse Wise was the name of the Pony Club the girls belonged to. Its home base was Pine Hollow.

Carole had left the house on time, but then she remembered Cam's message and ran back to call him, leaving her father waiting in the car. This time she got the Nelsons' machine and left word for Cam to call her. Frustrated, she stared out the window on the way over to Pine Hollow. It seemed as if she and Cam were fated never to talk to each other again.

"Cheer up, honey. You'll get in touch with him soon," Colonel Hanson said as he dropped her off.

Carole shook her head, smiling. Her father was as much of a mind reader as ever. Hurrying into the stable, she slipped in between Lisa and Stevie just as the meeting was starting.

Max had decided to have the Pony Clubbers themselves give presentations at the unmounted meetings because they would learn more that way. Today Polly Giacomin and Jackie were presenting a talk on winter grooming and horse care. They introduced the topic and then moved on to clipping.

"The decision to clip your horse depends on a lot of different things," Polly said. "Like, are you going to be riding a lot, is your horse kept inside or turned out, and do you want to keep the horse blanketed." While Jackie held up drawings of the different kinds of clips, Polly described them. "There's the full clip, when the whole coat is removed. Then there's the hunter clip, which is the whole coat minus the legs and a patch where the saddle goes. And then there's another kind called the blanket clip, which is just what it sounds like: You leave the hair on where a blanket would go and clip only the neck and belly." Polly paused to ask if there were any questions.

Stevie put her hand up. "I have one question. It's not exactly about clipping, it's about trimming."

"That's okay, what is it?" Jackie asked.

Looking first at Veronica and then back at Polly and Jackie, Stevie said, "I was wondering if you should keep a horse's whiskers trimmed even in the winter."

"Of course," Jackie said. "Unless you don't care at all about the horse's appearance, you should always keep the whiskers on the muzzle and around the ears trimmed."

Stevie nodded. "Okay, thanks. I just wanted to make sure."

Lisa and Carole knew exactly what Stevie was doing, but Veronica seemed oblivious. "We'll help," Lisa whispered.

"The next winter topic is blanketing. If you clip your horse, and a lot of times even if you don't, you'll want to keep him blanketed. The blanket can be anything from a light stable sheet to a heavy New Zealand rug with a liner," Jackie explained.

"That's right," Polly said. "And it's very important to know how to put the blanket on correctly and how to check to see if it's rubbing anywhere—"

"Excuse me," Lisa interrupted. "Isn't it also important to

57

check to make sure the blanket stays put? Can't a twisted sheet be annoying for the horse?"

"Absolutely. And not only annoying, it can be dangerous. If the horse gets a leg caught in one of the straps, he could panic," Polly said.

Satisfied, The Saddle Club looked at Veronica. But she still hadn't noticed that they were making digs at her care of Garnet. Suddenly she raised her hand. "Polly, I just thought of something. You should mention that for a really well-bred, high-strung horse like Danny, you should buy the best-quality blankets only. His coat is so fine that anything cheap would irritate him."

"By 'best-quality' she probably means a blanket with a huge 'Veronica diAngelo' monogram on it," Stevie muttered. Veronica was known for having every last item, from her blankets and saddle pads to her body brushes, monogrammed.

Thinking she would jump in while Veronica was paying attention to the meeting, Carole said loudly, "Didn't you mention something about turning your horse out even in the winter? Why is that important?" Out of the corner of her eye Carole saw Max, who'd been listening at the side of the room, raise his eyebrows. He was obviously surprised that Carole had asked such an easy question.

"We were just about to get to that," Jackie replied. "If

your horse is kept inside, it's very important to turn him out or exercise him regularly. There are a lot of reasons why. One is so that he doesn't get bored and develop vices—"

"You mean like cribbing and stall walking?" Stevie fairly shouted.

At Stevie's comment, The Saddle Club saw Max's eyes narrow as he, too, glanced at Veronica. But even though he had caught on to what the three of them were doing, Veronica had not. She sat more quietly than usual for the rest of the presentation, interrupting every so often to point out how perfectly she was taking care of Danny.

"The thing is, it's true," Carole murmured. "She *does* groom him and ride him every day. We've seen her!"

"Yeah. The more Daddy pays, the more time the horse deserves," said Stevie.

"While Garnet goes stale in her stall," Lisa added. "It's not fair!"

"So let's stop complaining and do something about it, okay?" Carole asked.

Stevie and Lisa nodded vigorously. So far they had done nothing to help Garnet—except show her to the perfect buyer and watch the perfect buyer walk away.

*   *   *

As SOON AS Polly and Jackie brought the lesson to a close, The Saddle Club rose and headed to the locker room to discuss Garnet.

"The way I see it, we just have to find another Katie Miller," Stevie said.

"Right. Someone who deserves to own Garnet and will take good care of her and appreciate her," Carole chimed in.

"Appreciate her? All that horse needs is a little discipline. A crop and spurs would do the trick," Lisa said in her best imitation of Henrietta Kingsley.

"Henrietta doesn't deserve a horse at all, let alone a nice one like Garnet," Stevie said.

Carole nodded. "I'll bet she isn't even a good rider. Why else wouldn't she have wanted to get on and try Garnet when she had the chance?"

"Easy," Stevie replied. "She suffers from Veronicitis. That's when you think that if you spend enough money on your horse and your clothes, not knowing how to ride won't matter."

"That's the whole problem," said Lisa. "We can't go to Veronica and tell her why Katie would make a better owner than Henrietta, because all Veronica cares about is selling her horse to the rich and famous Kingsleys."

"And even if we could somehow convince Veronica,

Katie's parents probably wouldn't let her buy Garnet anyway," Carole pointed out.

"But there are probably tons of other girls like Katie who would love to get Garnet . . ." Stevie let her voice trail off as she thought hard of the people she knew who rode. Finally she shook her head. "It's just, how do we find the tons of other girls?"

Stevie paused as Max knocked, then poked his head into the locker room. "I thought I heard talking—lucky for you I already asked the other Pony Clubbers to clean out the cobwebs from the rafters," he said.

"Say, Max," Stevie said before Max could think up another task, "do you know where the diAngelos have advertised Garnet?"

Looking slightly surprised by the question, Max told them he didn't think Garnet was advertised anywhere. "Other than the sign by the office, that is. The Kingsleys found out about Garnet through Mr. Kingsley's business connection with Veronica's father. Katie Miller heard about Garnet through a friend of hers who rides here. So I assume the diAngelos are relying on word of mouth."

Stevie nodded thoughtfully. "Well, Max," she said after a minute, "then you don't need to come up with any chores for The Saddle Club."

Max looked skeptical. "Oh, I don't?"

"Nope, we're going to be quite busy," Stevie said cheerfully.

"I see. And may I ask exactly what you'll be busy with?"

"You may ask, but"—Stevie paused dramatically—"unfortunately I won't be able to answer."

"I see," Max said again, eyeing her suspiciously.

"Rest assured, however, that whatever it is we're busy with is completely in line with all of the fundamentals of good horsemanship at Pine Hollow and in the greater equine universe beyond." Stevie grinned, looking pleased with herself.

"What the heck did you just say?" Max asked.

"I have absolutely no idea," Stevie said.

"Why doesn't that surprise me?" Max asked, but fortunately for the girls, he didn't seem to expect an answer.

"Don't touch that bologna!" Stevie's brother Chad yelled. The girls had adjourned to the Lakes' house to make plans. But first they had decided to satisfy their hunger. Unfortunately they had walked into the kitchen at the same moment that Chad, Michael, and Alex were satisfying *their* hunger. A mass of cold cuts, cheese, mayonnaise, mustard, lettuce, and tomatoes was spread out over the counter. The boys were eagerly cramming the food into pita pockets. Stevie had just attempted to filch a slice of bologna but had been caught in the act.

"I can't even have one piece?" she demanded.

Chad shook his head. "No way. One piece will turn into two, and then there'll be none left for us. Mom bought all this for us. Hear that? *Us.* Not you girls," Chad said, plucking the bologna slice out of Stevie's hand and shoving it into his mouth.

Carole and Lisa laughed. Stevie could get very angry at her brothers, and their antics were fun for outsiders to observe—as long as they stayed antics and didn't develop into knock-down-drag-out family feuds.

Stevie stared at Chad with contempt. Then her eyes lit up. "All right, fine; we'll skip the sandwiches and go right to dessert. I always was a fan of chocolate layer cake." With that Stevie ran to the refrigerator and grabbed the cake she'd mentioned, jealously guarding it with her body.

"No fair! Alex, grab the cake!" Chad yelled.

Alex went toward Stevie, but at the last second she handed the cake off to Carole. "Victory!" Stevie yelled as Carole did her best to hold the cake over her head.

A few minutes later, the girls were happily munching sandwiches up in Stevie's room, having exchanged half the cake for half the cold cuts with Stevie's brothers.

"I always did like the idea of the barter system," Stevie said, chewing contentedly.

"Yeah, but it's lucky Veronica can't barter Garnet away," Lisa said. "She'd probably trade her for a new saddle pad!" While she was eating, Lisa had gotten a legal pad and a pencil out of her bag and was jotting down a few notes.

"What have you got there, Lisa?" Carole asked.

"I was just trying to come up with ways we could advertise Garnet. Do you think we should run an ad in the local paper?" Lisa asked.

"Maybe as a last resort," Carole said. "But I think the fastest, cheapest, and probably the best way is just to hang signs around town. We've got to get cracking right away: The Kingsleys' vet could arrive any second, and we all know that Garnet isn't going to fail the vet check."

"You've got a point," Stevie said. "And so many people in Willow Creek ride that I'd be surprised if we didn't drum up some interest in a great horse like Garnet. You know what? I'll get some posterboard and some markers, and we can do the signs this minute."

"You have posterboard?" Lisa asked.

Stevie looked benevolently at her friend. "Lisa, darling, you must know by now that there's nothing Stephanie Lake's closet does not hold."

Carole and Lisa laughed. Stevie's closet was famous for being a bottomless pit of junk, but a lot of times the "junk" came in handy.

"So we just have to figure out how to get across what a great horse Garnet is, right?" Carole said.

Lisa nodded. "We've got to put in all the normal information you always see in ads," she said, "like height, breed, color, and experience." She scrawled on the pad for a minute. "Okay: Fifteen-point-one-hand purebred chestnut Arabian. That's the easy stuff."

"How about 'Amazingly talented show horse ready to win'?" Stevie suggested.

"That sounds like Garnet is an Olympic show jumper," Carole said flatly.

"I'm afraid I agree," Lisa said.

Carole continued, "I was thinking of something more like 'Has pony-clubbed successfully.' "

Stevie stood up from rummaging in the closet, posterboard and Magic Markers in hand. "Yeah, or: 'Has pony-clubbed successfully while ridden by biggest pain in Willow Creek,' " she suggested.

Carole gave her a withering glance, but Stevie was on a roll. "Or how about 'Attractive chestnut Arabian, formerly ridden by spoiled brat'?"

Lisa giggled. " 'For sale immediately: Horse that is too nice for present owner and desperate to escape!' "

" 'Wanted!' " Carole cried. " 'Anyone! Buy me now because nothing could be worse than belonging to Veronica diAngelo!' "

When they had finally stopped laughing and had gotten control of themselves again, Lisa made Carole and Stevie sit quietly while she thought. Then she recited the perfect description: " 'For sale: Attractive, fifteen-point-one-hand purebred chestnut Arabian. Has been shown and pony-clubbed successfully. Nice gaits, good jumper. Call the number below for more information.' "

When she was finished, Carole and Stevie clapped loudly. "I have just one question," Carole said. "Whose number are we planning to give?"

Lisa chewed on her lip, thinking. "Well, we can't give Veronica's, can we?"

"No. The whole point of our trying to sell Garnet is that Veronica doesn't care enough to find a good owner herself. If people start calling her, the diAngelos' maid will proba-bly answer and Veronica will never call them back," Car-ole said.

"And we can't give our numbers because we could be gone at school, so I guess it'll have to be Pine Hollow's," Stevie reasoned.

"All right, Pine Hollow's it is. We'll have to keep Max informed," Lisa reminded them.

"And tell him that we'd like to be the ones to show Garnet to the buyers," Carole added.

It took the better part of an hour for the three of them to copy the information onto the sheets of posterboard. When they had finished, the signs looked good—colorful and eye-catching.

Before leaving to hang the signs up, Carole and Lisa called home to let their parents know where they were. Carole's father told her Cam had called again.

"It was only about ten minutes ago," Colonel Hanson said. "So if I were you, I'd call him back from Stevie's. The poor guy has been trying to reach you for days."

Carole grinned at her father's sudden sympathy for Cam. She got the Nelsons' number from her father and called Cam right away. To her relief, this time he answered.

"Cam!"

"Carole!"

"I can't believe I actually got you," Carole said.

"I know—me neither, but I'm glad you did. How've you been?"

"Good—I mean, fine. I can't talk too long because I'm at my friend's and we're about to leave. But how about you? How've you been?"

There was a pause. Then Cam said, "I've been—I've been okay. Listen, I was hoping we could meet up this week. Are you free Monday afternoon? I have to ride first, but we could meet later."

"Sure, I'm free. Where do you want to go?"

"I don't know. You pick," Cam said.

Carole thought fast. "How about TD's? We go there for ice cream all the time—Stevie, Lisa, and I."

"That sounds great. Four o'clock at TD's, okay?" Cam asked.

"Four o'clock's fine," Carole replied. The two of them said their good-byes and hung up.

As soon as Carole put the receiver down, Stevie pounced. "Carole Hanson, did I hear the name 'Cam' in that phone call?"

Carole nodded, trying not to grin but failing. Even though Cam had sounded worried, she was thrilled to have a sort of date with him.

"And did I also hear TD's mentioned—" Stevie began.

"Stevie," Lisa interrupted, "how would you have heard Carole's conversation? That is, unless you were eavesdropping."

"Guilty as charged," Stevie said sheepishly. "But—"

Carole put a hand up. "I'll explain everything on the way."

*   *   *

TOGETHER THE GIRLS walked to the center of Willow Creek. They hung signs in the feed store, the tack shop, TD's; on a telephone pole; even on a park bench or two—anywhere they thought horsey people might see them. Carole explained the situation with Cam: that they had been playing phone tag and that he had sounded anxious when she spoke to him. Stevie and Lisa were sure Cam was just nervous about seeing her because he liked her.

"Anyway, everything will be clear on Monday afternoon, I guess," Carole said.

Saving one sign for Pine Hollow's bulletin board, the three of them headed home.

"We've done our best for Garnet," Lisa said. "Now we can only cross our fingers and hope."

AT NINE O'CLOCK Sunday morning, Stevie eagerly telephoned Carole, and they conference-called Lisa. "I just got off the phone with Max," Stevie explained breathlessly. "Somebody already saw one of the signs we put up yesterday and wants to look at Garnet today. His father is bringing him over."

"Great. And we're supposed to show Garnet?" Carole asked.

"Yup. Max was thrilled to give us the job from now on," Stevie replied.

"What about the Kingsleys? Have they been calling?" Lisa asked.

"So far, no. Max hasn't heard from them. Who knows? Maybe they found an Arabian whose bloodlines could be traced back to the year five hundred B.C.," Stevie joked. "Oh, wait, I forgot to tell you the catch: We have to have Garnet ready in an hour. Think we can do it?"

"I'll be out the door in five minutes," Carole promised.

"Whoever gets there first, start brushing," Lisa said, hanging up the phone and reaching for her jeans.

WORKING AS FAST as they could, the three girls barely had time to give Garnet a quick brush and smooth a few tangles out of her mane. As Lisa gave Garnet's hindquarters a final swipe with the rub rag, a small boy and his father came through the main door.

"Is this the horse we saw advertised in the ice cream parlor?" the man asked. Abruptly he pointed a finger at Garnet, who threw up her head in surprise.

"That's right," Lisa said. "This is Garnet. And who might you be?" she asked the little boy gently.

"I'm Jimmy Jones," the boy squeaked out. He looked down at his boots shyly.

"Have you been riding for a while, Jimmy?" Lisa asked.

"That's right," Mr. Jones answered, before Jimmy could

71

speak. "My son's eight and he's been taking lessons for a year now, haven't you Jim?" He gave his son an encouraging pat on the back.

Jimmy nodded. "I love riding. In my lessons I ride a pony called Soda Pop. She's a Shetland."

"My wife and I want to get Jimmy a horse for his birthday, which is next week," the father explained. "He's wanted a horse for as long as I can remember."

Lisa nodded and asked Jimmy if he would like to brush Garnet a little, but Jimmy hung back with his father.

Stevie and Carole exchanged glances. The situation was completely clear to them. Mr. Jones was well-meaning but knew nothing about horses. He wanted to make his son happy but obviously had no idea what kind of horse Jimmy needed. In fact, Jimmy didn't need a horse at all: He needed a nice, docile pony to boost his confidence. And while Garnet was well trained, she was also spirited. She wouldn't be above testing her rider to see if he could control her.

"This color is just the color horse that Jimmy wants," Mr. Jones said cheerfully. He reached out a hand to pat Garnet on the nose, but Garnet laid her ears back and sidled away. "Hey, she's got some spunk in her, doesn't she? Good. I like a horse with vitality. What do you think, Jimmy?"

"She's pretty," Jimmy said quietly. "But she's a lot bigger than Soda Pop."

"The way you're going to grow, you'll need a bigger horse in no time," Mr. Jones said.

While Lisa got Garnet saddled and bridled, Stevie and Carole conferred. "I'll take it from here, Lisa," Stevie said, extending a hand for Garnet's reins.

Relieved, Lisa handed Garnet to Stevie. She'd been wondering what she could say that would tactfully convince Mr. Jones that Garnet was all wrong for Jimmy. Stevie's confident tone made it obvious that she had a plan.

As soon as Stevie was mounted, it was clear what that plan was. Rather than trying to mask Garnet's acting up, as Carole had for Katie Miller, Stevie was doing her best to make Garnet look truly awful. As she warmed up, she gave Garnet a jab with her outside leg and acted surprised when Garnet bolted into a canter. Then she pretended that she couldn't get Garnet to slow down. "Whoa! Whoa!" she yelled, sitting back in the saddle and letting her reins flap.

Meanwhile, Lisa and Carole stood on either side of the boy's father and hammed it up. It was basically the same routine they had gone through with Henrietta, only they were more obnoxious this time because the boy's safety was at stake. "Wow, can this horse be terrible," Lisa said, pretending to address Carole but speaking across Mr. Jones.

"It's too bad that with so many people coming to look at her, nobody wants to buy her," Carole said.

"Well, if you got bucked off and trampled on, would *you* want to buy the horse?" Lisa demanded. "Anyway, looks like Stevie's got her going perfectly today."

As they looked out at the ring, Stevie headed Garnet toward a small jump. At the last minute she clearly told the horse to stop. Garnet slammed on the brakes, and Stevie fell onto her neck, shrieking. "This stupid horse! She never wants to jump!"

Carole and Lisa held their breaths, praying that the Joneses hadn't noticed Stevie's checking Garnet right before the jump.

"Didn't you advertise this horse as a good jumper?" Mr. Jones asked, sounding annoyed.

Lisa nodded. "Oh, she *is* a good jumper! Every few weeks when somebody actually gets her over a fence, she jumps it really well!"

That was the last straw for Mr. Jones. Taking his son by the hand, he thanked the girls—barely—and turned to go. "I don't want to buy my son a horse that won't jump. Jimmy needs a real performance animal, not some stable nag."

"Wait!" Carole called, running after them. She reached in her pocket, scribbled on a piece of paper, and handed it to Mr. Jones. Then she rejoined Lisa and Stevie.

"What did you give him?" Lisa asked.

"The name of a woman in the next town over who breeds Shetland and Welsh ponies—the kind of 'performance animal' Jimmy needs," Carole explained.

"Well, that makes me feel a little better," Stevie said. She gave Garnet an apologetic pat on the neck. "At least the day wasn't a total loss."

"But it was strike two for us trying to sell Garnet. We just *have* to find a buyer before the Kingsleys' vet gets here!" Lisa said.

THE SIGNS THAT The Saddle Club had put up were obviously doing their job. Monday afternoon after school the girls had another appointment with a potential buyer. Hurrying over to Pine Hollow, Carole hoped that the woman would be right for Garnet, but she was also distracted. Today was her TD's meeting with Cam, and she could hardly wait.

The minute she saw Lisa and Stevie getting Garnet ready, however, all thoughts of Cam fled her mind. Standing beside them was the tallest, fattest woman Carole had ever seen. The woman's hair was dyed a vivid red, and her fingernails were about three inches long and painted green. Next to the woman, Garnet looked like a ten-hand pony.

Regaining her composure, Carole went up to greet the woman and shake hands. "Pleased to meet you, honey," the woman said. "I'm Rose Marie Ambrosia Lee."

Before Carole could say hello, Rose Marie continued, "I was just telling your friends how thrilled I was to see the ad for this horse. You see, I'm looking for a new horse to ride in my costume parades."

"Costume parades?" Carole repeated. Lisa, Stevie, and Rose Marie all nodded.

"That's right. She dresses up like a Southern belle," Stevie said. Although she tried to make her voice sound normal, Carole could tell that Stevie was in as much shock as she was at the sight of the woman.

"I dress up like a Southern belle, you know antebellum, like. I wear a big hoopskirt and a hat with plumes and flowers—big plumes and flowers—and I decorate the horse to match my outfit. I've got lots of horse-rider combos that are just beautiful. There's my yellow Belle of the Ball outfit and of course my Scarlett O'Hara . . ."

As Rose Marie chatted, the girls groomed. Whenever two of them were on Garnet's off side, partially hidden from view, they would exchange horrified looks. The whole thing sounded frightening.

". . . anyway, my last horse, poor thing, I had to sell

77

him at auction because he developed chronic back prob-lems."

"At auction?" Carole mouthed to the others. Only peo-ple who didn't care at all about where their horses ended up sold them at auctions.

"How big a horse was he?" Stevie asked, fearing the worst.

"Oh, he was about the size of this here little ole dainty Arab. I always do like nice, dainty Arabs," Rose Marie said, smiling.

"Right, right," Stevie said. "Umm . . . listen, why don't you get better acquainted with Garnet while we get her tack, okay?"

Leaving Rose Marie cooing over Garnet, the three girls practically sprinted to the the tack room to conference.

"Chronic back problems?" Carole whispered. "No won-der—with Two-Ton Tessie on his back. The woman needs a much bigger horse—a warmblood, maybe, or a nice stocky quarter horse."

"Yeah, or a team of Clydesdales," Stevie added dryly.

"What should we do?" Lisa asked.

"You're doing the demo ride, right?" Steve asked.

Lisa nodded. "Yeah, but I don't think I should mess it up. She's probably a good enough rider to tell if I fake anything."

"True." Stevie paused. "All right, just go ahead with it, and I'll think up something."

When they rejoined the woman, Stevie mentioned what a flighty, nervous horse Garnet could be. "You can see by the way the wood on her stall is all chewed."

Rose Marie beamed. "Flighty? Nervous? That just about describes me! Sounds like Garnet and I are really going to hit it off."

Watching Lisa lead Garnet toward the ring, followed by Carole and Rose Marie, Stevie sighed. "It sure does," she muttered, "until poor Garnet collapses."

As luck would have it, Lisa's ride went better than ever. With all the buyers coming, Garnet was finally getting regular exercise. She had settled down a lot and behaved well. Lisa made sure not to show her off too much, but still, she knew the horse looked good. After fifteen minutes or so, she rode into the middle of the ring, dismounted, and reluctantly handed the reins over to Rose Marie. And after about another fifteen minutes, Rose Marie managed to get on. She had hopped around on the ground trying to get her foot in the stirrup until she finally heaved, panted, and groped her way up, aided at the last minute with a shove from behind by Carole.

"I do declare, it's marvelous up here. Nice little mare,

isn't she?" Still grinning from ear to ear, Rose Marie picked up the reins and asked Garnet for a walk.

If the situation hadn't been so desperate, The Saddle Club would have burst out laughing. Garnet's expression at having to carry Rose Marie Ambrosia Lee was pure indignance. "I thought you were going to do something," Lisa whispered to Stevie.

"Worried?" Stevie asked nonchalantly.

"Yeah. Worried that Rose Marie might want to try a trot," Lisa returned.

"Wait, she's getting off. Look," Carole said. The three of them looked. Having made one trip around the ring at a slow walk, Rose Marie seemed to have made up her mind. She slithered to the ground and came over to the girls.

"I've just about made up my mind, so unless there's any problem with the vet check, I'll—" Rose Marie started to say.

"Oh, we're so happy that you like Garnet!" Stevie gushed. "You know, I don't know if we mentioned this, but she even has parade experience."

"You're joshing me," Rose Marie said.

Stevie shook her head. "Nope. It's the truth. Last summer, at the—the—"

"The Founder's Day Parade!" Lisa blurted out.

"Right, it was the Founder's Day Parade," Stevie continued, shooting a look of gratitude at Lisa. "Anyway, Veronica, Garnet's owner, was riding her and they just looked great. Of course, when Garnet took off, Veronica's hair got a little mussed, but—"

"Took off? Why did she take off?" Rose Marie demanded.

Carole jumped in to back up Stevie. "She kept spooking at the people on the sidelines and finally she just went crazy, I guess, and she took off and—"

"—and ended up trampling a float of senior citizens and war veterans, but it wasn't that bad because only a few of them were injured, and Veronica only got a minor concussion, so you know what they say, all's well that ends well," Stevie finished triumphantly. "So, as I was saying, we're so happy that—"

Rose Marie held up a green-nailed hand. "Listen, kids, I think I'm going to have to think this one over. Sorry about that. It's just that I don't want to do anything hasty, you know what I mean? But look, thanks a lot, and I'll be in touch."

Stevie, Lisa, and Carole shook Rose Marie's hand and forced themselves to be silent while the woman made her way from the ring. When she was safely gone, they each breathed a sigh of relief.

"I don't know whether I should cheer that we averted

another disaster or cry that we're back to square one," Carole said.

"I'd cheer if I were you," Stevie said, her eyes lighting up.

"You would?" Carole asked.

"Naturally. You wouldn't want to get all puffy-eyed before your date with Cam," Stevie teased, ducking as Carole brandished a crop at her.

EVEN THOUGH STEVIE had been kidding, Carole quickly checked her appearance in the ladies' room mirror at TD's while she waited for Cam. She pulled a little piece of straw from her hair and tucked in her shirt. She didn't look half bad for having come right from Pine Hollow.

In her eagerness to be on time, Carole had arrived ten minutes early. A few seconds after she sat down at a booth, Cam walked in. Carole waved him over. "Guess we're both running early today, huh?" she asked.

"Hi, Carole; yeah, I guess we are," Cam said, sitting down with her.

Although he greeted her warmly, Carole noticed that Cam looked distracted, even solemn. For a few minutes the conversation was awkward. To have something to say, Carole began to tell him about all the people who had come to Pine Hollow to look at Garnet. She described Rose Marie,

Jimmy Jones, and then Katie Miller, whom they had liked so much.

"But she sounds perfect," Cam said, perking up.

"She is perfect. The problem is that Garnet was anything but. Katie was the first person who saw her and Garnet looked terrible and acted worse. Katie still liked her, but her parents didn't want to buy their daughter a neglected-looking horse who acted up," Carole concluded.

"So what you have to do now is find another Katie, right?" Cam asked.

Carole nodded. "Yes, but there's a catch." Briefly she filled him in on Henrietta Kingsley. "The worst thing is that the Kingsleys said they would definitely buy Garnet unless she failed the vet check, which, of course, she won't." Carole stopped talking as the realization hit her again: It was just a matter of time before Henrietta got Garnet, unless The Saddle Club could intervene. She told Cam what she was thinking.

"A matter of time?" Cam repeated.

Carole nodded glumly.

"Listen, Carole. . . ." Cam paused awkwardly and looked at Carole. "I—I hate to say this, but I have to tell you about something else that's kind of a matter of time, too."

Carole frowned. Cam was not making much sense. "What do you mean?" she asked.

All in a rush, Cam blurted out, "My dad got a promotion and we're moving!"

Carole didn't know what to say. "You are? Where? When?" she asked, hoping her voice didn't sound as shocked as she felt.

"Yeah, Dad got transferred to California, and we're leaving for Los Angeles as soon as the sale on our house goes through," Cam said quietly.

"But what about Duffy?" Carole asked.

Cam half smiled. "I'm glad you asked. That's the only good part. Duffy's coming with us, and I'll be able to keep him at the Los Angeles Equestrian Center. It's a fantastic place to train, and I'll be able to ride in great weather all year round. So I'm glad about that."

"That's super," Carole said enthusiastically. Then she stopped and looked down at her hands, not knowing what to add.

"That part is super," Cam agreed. "But the thing is, I'll really miss Virginia, and especially you, Carole. I feel like I was just getting to know you. I wanted to see you in person today because I didn't want to tell you over the phone, but—but we're leaving next week. I'm not sure I'll be able to see you again."

Carole was stunned. Her head seemed to be reeling. She knew that she and Cam had never really been girlfriend and boyfriend, so why did his news hurt her so much? The simple truth was that she really liked Cam—she liked being around him. Now she would never get a chance to get to know him better. Looking up at him, Carole kept a brave face. There was nothing else she could do.

8

CAROLE WAS STILL brooding over Cam's news when she arrived at Pine Hollow the next day for the Tuesday-afternoon lesson. She couldn't believe she wasn't going to be meeting him for trail rides or running into him at shows and Pony Club events in the spring. While she groomed Starlight, she kept going over the conversation at TD's. It had been great to hear Cam say he was going to miss her, but terrible that he would have to miss her in the first place!

As Carole put down her currycomb and picked up a body brush, Stevie and Lisa descended upon her and Starlight. "Carole, guess what! Somebody else is coming to look at Garnet after the lesson!" Lisa announced.

"And this time she sounds normal. I talked to her myself over the phone," said Stevie.

"Yeah, she's supposed to be very experienced," Lisa added.

"That's great," Carole said, trying to sound enthusiastic. It wasn't fair to Lisa and Stevie for her to lose interest in The Saddle Club project. And anyway, she needed some good news. "But, wait, what about . . . ?" Carole paused, raising her eyebrows at Veronica, who was talking to a man down the aisle.

"Oh, that's all taken care of," Lisa explained. "She said if we wanted to do her dirty work, we were welcome to it."

"She calls selling her old horse 'dirty work'?" Carole asked, shaking her head disapprovingly. Even though they all knew how bad Veronica could be, sometimes she still said things they could hardly believe.

Lisa nodded. "Her words exactly. And she said it was probably a waste of time because she was sure the Kingsleys would be sending a vet to check Garnet any moment."

"Who's she talking to, anyway?" Stevie asked.

Lisa shrugged. "Search me. But I think we're about to find out."

As Veronica brushed by them on her way to Danny's

stall, she shot them all a look of pity. "I would ask if any of you wanted to talk to the special farrier I've hired, but his rates are probably too high for you. It's lucky nothing's too good for Danny, because special horses have very specific shoeing requirements, you know." She paused and smiled sweetly. "Or, actually, maybe you don't: You three ride such ordinary horses."

At Veronica's words, Stevie nearly flew into a fury. The worst thing was that there was nothing they could say. In the past, when Veronica had bragged about Garnet, they could remind her that their ordinary horses had beaten her purebred Arabian on countless occasions. But if Danny went over as well at shows as he did in lessons, it might be a very different story. How could they compete with the perfect horse? "I'd love to see Danny do one little thing wrong. Veronica would probably fall off!" Stevie muttered. " 'Ordinary horses'! If Belle heard that, she'd go on strike for a month."

"So would Prancer—either that or she'd take a chunk out of Danny's perfect coat," Lisa said. "And I can't say I'd blame her." She and Stevie looked at Carole to see how she would defend Starlight, but Carole was quietly brushing the gelding's bay coat. She hardly seemed to have heard what Veronica had said. Lisa and Stevie exchanged concerned glances. It wasn't like Carole to space out, at least not around the stables.

"Carole, is anything wrong?" Lisa asked gently.

"Yeah, you seem like you're in another world," Stevie added.

Carole stopped grooming and looked up at them. To her surprise, she felt her eyes well up with tears. When she had choked them back, she explained, haltingly, about Cam. It took a while because she kept having to bite her lip. Lisa and Stevie were full of sympathy.

"I can't imagine how miserable I would be if Phil moved away," Stevie said glumly, referring to her longtime boy-friend.

Sniffing hard, Carole thanked them for listening. "You'd better hurry and get Belle and Prancer ready. The lesson starts in five minutes."

"But what about you?" Lisa asked.

"Yeah," Stevie said, "are you sure you're going to be all right?"

When Carole nodded, they each gave her a quick hug and went to tack up. "If anything will cheer Carole up, it's riding," Stevie predicted.

LISA AND STEVIE had planned to talk to Carole more after the lesson. They wanted to find out the details of Cam's move. But as soon as they had put their horses away, it was time to get Garnet out again: The new prospective owner had arrived. Luckily Carole seemed to be in better spirits. In the lesson Max had said that Starlight was listening to Carole better and that had helped.

To the delight of The Saddle Club, the new buyer was dressed in normal clothes for trying out a horse: well-broken-in boots and casual breeches. She was a young woman, about the right height for Garnet, and very talkative. In fact, she seemed more interested in her own qualifications than in Garnet's. As soon as Carole had finished relating Garnet's experience, the woman launched into a long description of her own skills. "So, anyway, I've showed all over the country in hunters, jumpers, dressage, and equitation, and I also do three-day events when my schedule permits—"

"Wow," Lisa breathed, "you must be amazing. I can't imagine doing all of those—"

"—and of course I do combined driving and long-distance trail riding and ride western. I do gymkhanas, vaulting"—here the woman paused for breath and beamed at the three girls—"I guess you could say 'the works,' huh?"

Lisa looked completely enthralled by the woman's list of riding activities. Anyone who did all those things must be decent—or better than decent. "Did you hear that? She sounds perfect," she whispered to Stevie and Carole as the woman leaned over to run a hand down Garnet's leg.

Obediently Garnet picked up her hoof, as she had been taught to do when someone squeezed her foreleg. Instead of examining the horse's hoof, the woman dropped the leg like a hot potato. "Oh, my gosh!" she exclaimed. "She's trying to kick!"

"Is there something wrong?" Carole asked anxiously. She thought she had heard something about kicking, but Garnet was a good-natured mare, and that was one vice she definitely did not have.

"Wrong? Oh, no. I don't think so. She seems fine to me." The woman gave a weak smile. "Did I mention that I also ride sidesaddle?"

"No, you didn't! Wow, I've always wanted to learn," Lisa said. "Here, why don't you brush Garnet a little to get to know her."

The woman stared at the currycomb Lisa handed her as if it would bite. "Oh, right, sure—good idea."

Stevie and Carole exchanged glances: Something was fishy about the woman. First she'd freaked out when Garnet picked up a hoof, and then she didn't seem to know what to do with a currycomb. It didn't mesh with the experience she claimed to have. And anyway, why would anyone as good as she made herself sound be interested in a nice, normal horse like Garnet? If the woman could do all the things she said she could, why wasn't she out looking for some wonder horse? And, Carole thought suspiciously, why was she attempting to use the hard rubber currycomb on Garnet's face?

All during the demonstration ride, Carole tried to figure out what was strange about the woman. Carole didn't pull any tricks while she warmed Garnet up, although she didn't try to make Garnet look spectacular. She just went through the normal walk, trot, canter, and a few low jumps before handing over the reins.

As soon as the woman got on, all became clear: She could barely ride. She was either horrible—or a stark beginner. She was completely ham-handed, she leaned on the reins for balance, and her legs flopped everywhere. When she posted to the trot, she rose way too high in the saddle and stayed up forever.

"You can see half of Pine Hollow between her seat and the saddle," Carole whispered to her friends.

"Yeah, isn't that what they call hang time?" Stevie joked.

"No, 'hanging' is what she's doing on Garnet's mouth," Carole murmured.

Lisa looked from the woman to her friends. Suddenly it was all sinking in. She felt silly for being so trusting, but she couldn't have imagined that someone would be stupid enough to lie about her riding level. What if Garnet had been truly high-strung and difficult? The woman wouldn't have stood a chance. "Guess I was a little naive about all her 'experience,' huh? Look at poor Garnet."

Stevie and Carole looked. Garnet was coping, but she was too sensitive a horse to put up with the bad handling for long. Besides, The Saddle Club knew, she shouldn't have to. They were about to take votes on who should say something when Garnet took matters into her own hands —or hooves—and let out a frustrated buck, unseating the woman, who shrieked at the top of her lungs. As quickly as she could, she slithered back into the saddle. Then, almost as quickly, she jumped to the ground. Or at least she tried to jump, but at the last minute her toe got caught in the stirrup iron and she tumbled backward into the dirt. Stevie, Lisa, and Carole ran over to reassure her.

Springing to her feet and brushing herself off, the woman exclaimed, "I don't need to try her anymore—I love her! How much did you say you wanted?"

The Saddle Club stared in shock. In their few days of showing Garnet, they had realized something for the first time, and it was alarming: People were willing to buy horses for all the wrong reasons. This woman seemed ready to buy Garnet out of embarrassment at her poor performance! Unbelievably, she had fished in her pocket and come up with a blank check.

"You w-want to *buy* her?" Carole asked. "You mean, like, to *ride?*"

"No, I want to buy her to put in the garden and grow," the woman snapped. Having made a fool of herself, she had now turned rude. "Of course to ride. What did you think?"

"I—I—," Carole sputtered, unable to come up with a response.

"We just thought that with all the high-level, different kinds of riding you do, you might need a more advanced horse than Garnet. She's just a good, low-key Pony Club mount," Stevie said, coming to Carole's aide. It never hurt to try reverse psychology.

"Nope. I'm sure she'll do fine." There was a pause as the woman gave The Saddle Club a fake smile—and The Saddle Club continued to stare back in utter shock.

"So, you're saying you want to pay for her now?" Lisa questioned.

"That's usually what a check is for, isn't it?"

"Yes—oh, yes," Lisa replied. Then, trying to sound as innocent as possible, she added, "I guess you don't, ah, know about vet checks, then?"

The woman frowned at her. "Vet checks?" she said.

"Oh, it's nothing—just a silly little habit some people have of making their veterinarian check a horse before they buy it," Lisa said hurriedly.

"Oh yeah?" the woman said. "Maybe I'd like to hear more about this silly little habit."

"It's nothing—really. Garnet is fine, absolutely fine," Lisa said, looking up at the ceiling and then down at her feet.

"Fine? You're sure?" the woman demanded.

Lisa nodded. "Definitely. One hundred percent fine. No problems at all. No medical problems."

The woman stepped back and narrowed her eyes at Lisa. "Maybe I should have a vet check if—"

"It's really not necessary. Forget I even mentioned it. Look, why don't you just write that check out, and Garnet will be yours before you can say—"

The woman put her hands on her hips. "Wait just a minute here, young lady. I'm not an idiot, you know. I see perfectly well what's going on."

"You do?" Lisa asked nervously.

"Of course. You're trying to pull the wool over my eyes. You know, you may feel that just because you and your little friends ride in the Pony Club that you can take advantage of people. Think that's pretty funny, huh? Well, let me tell you something, I never even *wanted* to be in the

95

Pony Club! I despise the Pony Club! For all I care, the Pony Club could drop off the face of the earth, okay?"

"Okay," Lisa said meekly.

"So, you can just keep your Pony Club and your vet checks and your stupid horse, too, okay? Okay? I know when I'm being duped!"

Lisa nodded. She, Carole, and Stevie watched the now red-faced woman stalk out of the ring. At the gate, the woman turned. "Did I mention I go foxhunting in Ireland every year?" she yelled.

SEVERAL MINUTES AFTER she had gone, The Saddle Club was still standing silently, staring at one another in disbelief. "What exactly went on here?" Carole finally asked.

"I can't say that I know," Lisa replied.

"Basically, another one just bit the dust," said Stevie. "And it's back to the drawing board."

"Right," said Carole. "Thank goodness Garnet survived."

"Well, naturally: She is one hundred percent fine. No medical problems at all," Lisa joked, raising her hands to high-five Carole and Stevie.

EVEN THOUGH LISA had saved the day at the last minute, the girls were frustrated. It didn't help that while they untacked Garnet and put her away, they could hear Veronica driving the farrier nuts with her overly detailed instructions about Danny.

"Are you sure you're not using the rasp too much?" Veronica asked, anxiously examining Danny's off-fore foot.

The farrier took a deep breath. It was obvious that he was trying to keep his temper in check. "Yes, I'm sure," he said testily.

"Remember he needs pads on all four feet, not just the front," Veronica whined.

"You've told me that three times already," the farrier said.

Veronica shrugged. "Just watching out for my baby," she said. She turned to stroke Danny, cooing baby talk at him. "My wittle bumpkin, my wittle sweetheart needs his tootsies to be perfect, don't you, Danny?"

"Is it me, or is the air in here *nauseating?*" Stevie asked.

"Danny doesn't seem thrilled, either," Lisa pointed out. It was true: Once again, the beautiful horse was more or less ignoring Veronica. He had a bored expression on his face, and his ears flopped back lazily.

"I guess he's not the touchy-feely type," Carole mused.

"Hello, girls, how's it going?" The Saddle Club turned to greet Mrs. Reg, who had emerged from the office. Max Regnery's mother was one of their favorite people at Pine

Hollow, even if she did tell long, sometimes cryptic stories. Today she didn't pause to chat, but went directly to speak to Veronica.

"A message for you, dear: I just returned a call to the Kingsleys' vet in Kentucky. He's going to fly in tomorrow to check Garnet."

Stevie, Lisa, and Carole looked at one another in horror. "We've got to do something," Carole whispered.

Stevie's mouth tightened into a determined line. "We will." Before they could guess what she had in mind, Stevie motioned Carole and Lisa into the empty office. She searched the desk, but it was bare: There wasn't a phone number to be found. Then, all at once, she looked at her friends, grinned, picked up the receiver, and hit Redial.

"BUT WHAT IF the whole plan doesn't work?" Lisa asked. She, Stevie, and Carole were gathered in the locker room on the following afternoon. Although they had gone over the plan a hundred times, it was hard to believe it would really go off as planned.

"Trust me," Stevie said confidently, yanking on her breeches, "we've already done the hard part. Besides, remember who thought this up: yours truly. And don't my schemes always work?"

"No," Carole said, grinning. "A lot of times your schemes completely backfire, and we get into trouble and you have to get us out."

"And if we don't pull this off, Veronica will have a cow," Lisa said.

Now it was Stevie's turn to grin. "Right, but if we do pull it off, then she *won't* have a horse! Or, at least, she won't have two horses! Ha ha, two horses, get it?"

Carole and Lisa rolled their eyes and went back to pulling on their boots. It was nice that Stevie was so confident about her plan. They just wished they felt the same. Instead their stomachs were churning the way they did the night before horse shows. But it was too late to back out now.

"Ready, crew?" Stevie asked.

"Ready, captain," Carole replied, saluting smartly. Now that they were committed, they might as well do their best to follow Stevie's plan.

"Ready," said Lisa. The three of them clicked their heels together and marched to Garnet's stall.

While Lisa took Garnet out and cross tied her, Carole and Stevie got a grooming kit and a pair of clippers from the tack room. "All right, troops: Attack," Stevie commanded. And all three of them attacked, giving Garnet the grooming of her life.

First Carole went at the chestnut coat with a rubber currycomb, digging up big clouds of dried sweat and dirt. She brushed the dirt away with a body brush, then set about detangling every hair in Garnet's tail. It actually felt good for her to have something to throw herself into so that she wouldn't think about Cam too much. The night before at dinner, she had told her father the news. Colonel Hanson's advice had been to keep as busy as she could.

While Carole curried and brushed, Lisa combed Garnet's mane and forelock. Then she pulled the mane until it was the proper length, wrapping the long hairs around her fingers and tearing them, a few strands at a time. As Lisa knew, the pulling didn't hurt because horses have so few nerves at the base of their manes. Stevie picked out the mare's hooves, following up with a coat of polish. All three of them shined her with rub rags until they were panting. A determined air had settled over them, and they worked in silence. Finally Carole plugged in the clippers and trimmed Garnet's muzzle, bridle path, and ears.

"You know," Carole said when she had finished and turned off the clippers, "we should hire ourselves out at shows. She looks like she's ready for a national championship."

"Talk about 'before' and 'after'!" Lisa exclaimed with pride. Garnet's appearance had improved so much that she looked like a different horse—which, after all, was the point. What was more, she seemed to relish all the attention. She stood still and looked happy and alert, with her ears pricked up.

"Before we congratulate ourselves too much, we still have to do something about her stall," Stevie reminded them. In a jiffy Lisa was raking Garnet's bedding to cover up the mare's pacing habit. Meanwhile Stevie and Carole smoothed out the chewed wood with sandpaper. It wouldn't look perfect, but it would at least camouflage her faults.

"My, aren't we industrious today." Max paused to survey the girls' handiwork. "You really gave Garnet the royal treatment, didn't you?"

When The Saddle Club nodded, Max asked, "Any special reason for all the hard work? I mean, Garnet's pretty much sold to the Kingsleys."

"Just trying to be helpful," Stevie said firmly.

Max looked doubtful but didn't press the point. "Speaking of the Kingsleys, where is Veronica? Have you seen her? She was supposed to meet me and the Kingsleys' vet ten minutes ago. And neither of them are here."

Stevie mocked surprise. "Really? That's funny. Because I heard that the vet couldn't come. Something about an emergency in Kentucky."

Max raised his eyebrows. "Oh? Funny how I'm always the last one to know."

"I think Veronica said that the vet was going to have to reschedule for next week or something. Yes, that was definitely it," Stevie said.

Though he seemed surprised, Max thanked Stevie for letting him know, shook his head wearily, and headed off down the aisle.

"At least that's what Veronica thinks," Stevie murmured when he was safely out of earshot.

"And you're *sure* Veronica believed it?" Lisa asked.

"Positive," Carole said. "Why wouldn't she? I know from working with Judy Barker that vets have emergencies all the time. Horses get colic, turn up lame—the works. And if they're valuable, the owners get frantic very fast. Besides, Lisa, you were completely convincing."

"Really?" Lisa asked.

Carole nodded. "I knew you could act, but I didn't know you could fake a Kentucky accent. Pretending to be the vet's secretary and calling both Veronica and Henrietta— that was great!"

"Hey, don't forget *I* was the one who called the Kingsleys' vet back and told him not to come. That was pretty good acting too, wasn't it?" Stevie asked.

"To be honest, your Mrs. Reg imitation could use a little work. Remind me to give you a few pointers sometime when—" Lisa didn't get a chance to finish her sentence because Stevie had smothered her in hay.

Carole, however, stopped the skirmish before it could really get going. They had worked too hard on Garnet to mess her up now. Carefully they returned the horse to her stall and covered her with a clean, white stable sheet. She looked magnificent—much, much better than she had the week before.

"I think all the exercise she got in the demonstration rides is doing her good, too. She isn't hyper anymore," Lisa said.

"After meeting Henrietta Kingsley, Jimmy Jones, Rosie Lee, and the jack-of-all-trades woman, I'm surprised she has any life left in her," Carole said, laughing. It was truly shocking, the kind of people who had turned up thinking they needed a "fifteen-point-one-hand purebred Arabian."

Carole reached over the stall door and gave the mare a good pat. "Just do your stuff, Garnet," she told her. "You have to make this work, too." Garnet stepped forward and gave Carole a friendly nuzzle. She was the picture of good care, attentive but relaxed.

"That's right," Stevie warned sternly. "We didn't do all this work for nothing, you know." In response, Garnet whiffled softly through her nose. "Humph, I'll believe it when I see it," Stevie said.

"So now all we have to do is wait, huh?" Lisa asked.

Carole glanced at her watch. "Yes, and if all goes according to schedule, we shouldn't have to wait long."

10

BEFORE LONG, THE Saddle Club heard the sound of a car pulling into the Pine Hollow driveway. A peek through the window revealed that it was the car they'd been waiting for. Keeping their fingers crossed, the girls went to the stable door to greet Katie Miller and her parents.

"I'm so glad you called me!" Katie exclaimed. "I can't wait to see the new horse for sale. None of the other horses we've looked at have seemed even half as nice as the first one I saw here." As she spoke, Katie gave her parents a slightly sulky look. Mr. and Mrs. Miller crossed their arms over their chests and glared back.

Noticing Katie's look, Lisa felt her hopes rise. So Katie

really had liked Garnet as much as she seemed to! That was the main thing. Now if only the rest of the plan worked as well . . .

"I can't believe the lies some people will tell you when they're trying to sell you a horse," Katie said. She was chatting happily as The Saddle Club led her and her parents down the aisle. "One person advertised an 'attractive, quiet gelding.'"

"Let me guess," Carole said. "He was anything but."

"Unless you call being Roman-nosed and swaybacked 'attractive' and taking off with me three times 'quiet,'" Katie joked. "And then there was an 'experienced hunter' who had never jumped outside a ring before and wouldn't walk through water."

"Isn't there a law against false advertising?" Lisa asked.

"If there is, then I've met a bunch of criminals," said Katie. "I guess the only good part about looking at all these horses is that I've gotten pretty good at riding all kinds of them. Speaking of which, who's the new horse for sale at Pine Hollow?"

The Saddle Club looked a little shamefaced, but Stevie brazened it out. "This way," she said, leading the group straight past Garnet's stall. As they went by, Garnet poked her nose over the door with interest. "Hey, girl," Stevie said, giving her a cursory pat.

Katie's eyes grew huge. She sucked in her breath. "Isn't this Garnet?" she asked.

Stevie nodded. "Sure is. The horse we wanted you to see is right over—"

"Oh, look at her, Mom! Dad! Remember her? Remember Garnet? See how pretty she is!" Katie had stopped outside the stall to admire the chestnut mare.

Carole and Lisa exchanged hopeful glances: Garnet was playing her role perfectly. She pricked her ears up at the Millers, turning her fine Arabian head toward them.

Mr. Miller peered at Garnet with curiosity. Mrs. Miller pushed her glasses up on her nose to get a better look. "You don't mean that this is the horse you tried here before?" Mrs. Miller said finally.

"Of course it is, Mom. I'd know that nice face anywhere," Katie gushed. She reached out to scratch Garnet behind the ears.

"But she looks so different," Mr. Miller protested.

"She's just groomed better, that's all," Katie responded. "I knew she'd look this good with some care."

"She seems calmer, too, dear," Mrs. Miller murmured.

Stevie let them admire Garnet for a few more minutes before dragging the three of them to look at the other horse "for sale." She knew she had to play it carefully and let Garnet's transformation sink in slowly. "Here he is,"

she said, with as much enthusiasm as she could muster.
"Here's Patch."

The Millers looked a bit surprised at the old, stocky
pinto. Around Pine Hollow, Patch was known for being a
great lesson horse for beginners. He was slow and arthritic,
so he never scared even the youngest kids. Of course, he
was totally wrong for Katie—something that Stevie, Lisa,
and Carole were banking on. If she happened to take a
liking to him—well, that was one "if" they didn't dare
imagine.

"He looks . . . sweet," Katie said, a doubtful note in
her voice. Patch was at least a hand shorter than Garnet,
whom Katie had fit perfectly.

"Great, we'll have him saddled up in no time," Stevie
said as the three of them went to work.

"Are you sure you want to try him, dear?" Mrs. Miller
asked quietly. "I mean, he looks nice, but didn't you want
something more . . . spirited?"

Before Katie could respond, Stevie jumped in. "We
know how important getting a safe horse is for you, and I
can tell you, Patch is as safe as they come."

"He ought to be, at nineteen," Lisa added cheerfully.

Katie smiled wanly. It was obvious that she was very
disappointed but didn't want to be rude. "Sure I'll try him.
It can't hurt," she said. As she took the reins and led Patch

out toward the ring, Mr. and Mrs. Miller dropped back to confer about something. The Saddle Club pretended not to notice.

Patch behaved the same as he always did: He walked and trotted at a snail's pace and had to be coaxed into a canter. He wasn't exactly disobedient, it just took him about halfway around the ring to summon up the energy to do what his rider asked him. Before long, Katie was huffing and puffing from having to use her legs constantly.

"So far, so good," Lisa murmured cautiously to Carole and Stevie as Katie rode by, clucking and exaggerating her aids to try to get Patch to wake up.

Carole nodded. "For a minute I was afraid that Patch might betray us and act peppy today!" she whispered. "But I shouldn't have worried." Just at that moment Patch, feeling Katie sit back in the saddle a fraction, broke instantly to a walk.

"I know. Imagine Max's face if we had to tell him we'd sold a horse for him—his best lesson horse!" said Lisa.

The three of them fell silent as Katie rode over. "Thanks for letting me try him, but—"

"Oh, but wait! You haven't jumped him," Stevie said. "He's just as safe and steady over fences as he is on the flat —really!"

"I'm sure he is. It's not that, it's—"

"Great. Trot the cross rail a couple of times," Stevie ordered.

Katie opened her mouth to say something but seemed to think better of it. Her good manners prevented her from arguing with Stevie. She headed Patch to the little jump, picking up a trot.

"You're turning into a regular drill sergeant," Carole remarked.

"I just had to make her jump him once," Stevie confessed, nodding her head in the direction of Katie's parents. "That way they'll see that 'safe' doesn't have to mean 'slow.' "

"Are you sure it wasn't for entertainment purposes?" Lisa questioned skeptically.

"Are you kidding?" Stevie asked, feigning shock.

Meanwhile Patch lumbered over the cross rail, not even breaking to a canter on the landing. After two more jumps, Katie turned him toward The Saddle Club again. This time she had a determined look on her face. "Listen, I've tried him enough, and he's just not right for me," she said. As if she were afraid that Stevie might try to make her ride Patch more, she dismounted right away. Then, just as determinedly, she waved her parents over. "Mom, Dad, this horse is safe all right, but he's a beginner's horse. And I'm no expert, but I'm no beginner either."

"We know he's not right for you, Katie. Your mother and I have been talking, and we think—"

Inside her coat pocket, Stevie crossed her fingers.

Before her father could say what he thought, Katie interrupted. "Just please let me finish and then you can say what you want. Since we're here already, I want to try Garnet one more time. I mean, please may I try Garnet one more time?"

"That's exactly what I was going to suggest," Mr. Miller said, looking relieved. Without waiting for The Saddle Club, the three Millers walked off in the direction of Garnet's stall.

After a quick consultation, The Saddle Club split up. Carole went to put Patch away, Stevie went to supervise Garnet's tacking up, and Lisa stayed behind in the ring to set up some jumps. That way, she figured, Katie wouldn't be able to resist going around the course at least once.

The rest of the afternoon went like clockwork. From the minute Katie got on Garnet, she had a huge smile on her face. She walked, she trotted, she cantered. She practiced halting and leg-yielding, rode twenty-meter circles, and hand-galloped. Then she started to jump. Garnet flew over the fences easily, and at Katie's request The Saddle Club raised them a few inches for a second go-round. Not until Katie had ridden over the course three times did she realize that she'd been riding for more than an hour and that Garnet might be getting tired. "I'm having too much fun," she admitted. She loosened the reins to let Garnet cool down and gave the mare a hearty pat on the neck.

Mr. and Mrs. Miller had huge smiles on their faces, too, as they watched their daughter put Garnet through her paces.

"I've seen that look before," Stevie said. "It's the proud parent look. And once you get the proud parent look, you're home free. Katie'll be able to ask for whatever she wants."

"What's that, one of the ten cardinal rules of horse selling?" Lisa asked.

Stevie shook her head. "No, one of the ten cardinal rules of living in the Lake household. It's kind of the same principle as 'Bring home an A/Get to stay up late watching TV.' "

"Boy, I wish I'd known about that one," Lisa said wistfully. Stevie and Carole laughed. If the rule had applied in the Atwood household, Lisa would have been able to watch TV until midnight every night of her life.

It seemed like forever before Katie finally rode over to The Saddle Club and dismounted. The Millers joined the group of girls at once. There was a pause as Katie rolled up her stirrups and loosened the girth. The Saddle Club didn't dare look at one another. By sabotaging the Kingsleys and luring Katie back to Pine Hollow to see the "new and improved" Garnet, they had played every card in their hand. If Stevie's plan failed, there was nothing they could do except spend the next month trying to get out of the trouble they had created. But more than the trouble, they were worried about Garnet. She and Katie deserved each other: They would make a great team, learning from each other's faults and appreciating each other's strengths. And yet it all came down to what Katie said about—

"Mom? Dad?" Katie began. She draped an arm over Garnet's neck. She took a deep breath and looked up at her parents solemnly. "Please, please, please, please, please, can I have her?"

11

"FIVE 'PLEASES,' HUH?" Mr. Miller said. "Well, in that case— Yes!"

"We agreed while you were riding: She's all yours, dear." Mrs. Miller added.

Katie squealed and flung her arms around her parents. Then the whole family turned and gave Garnet a hug. Then Katie hugged Stevie, Lisa, and Carole. Then she hugged her parents again. And then The Saddle Club hugged one another. They had pulled it off!

"Provided, of course, that she passes the vet check," Mrs. Miller reminded her daughter.

"Can we call Dr. Weicker right now to see if she can come tomorrow?" Katie pleaded.

"Is that Dr. Jacqueline Weicker?" Carole asked.

Katie nodded. "Yes. My instructor says she's one of the best vets in the county."

"I've heard the same," Carole said enthusiastically. "I know her name from a vet I worked with, Judy Barker. Judy mentioned that she was excellent." Lisa and Stevie could see that Katie had risen even higher in Carole's eyes because she was going to use a vet whom Judy had recommended.

Now that the big decision had been made, the Millers and The Saddle Club got very friendly and talkative. The Millers explained that they were building a small, two-stall barn on their property, but for now Garnet would live at Katie's instructor's stable.

"We didn't want to take her home prematurely," Mr. Miller said. "And until the barn is finished and the two acres are all fenced in, we wouldn't think of keeping a horse there."

"You should see the plans. It's going to be the most perfect little barn," Katie said.

Then The Saddle Club wanted to hear all about the Irish setters that Mr. and Mrs. Miller raised.

"Don't get them started—they'll never stop," Katie

116

warned kiddingly. It was clear that she was very close to her parents, since the three of them could joke around. It was also clear from the way the Millers described their dogs that even though they weren't horse people, they obviously loved animals. There was no doubt in Lisa's, Stevie's, or Carole's minds that Garnet would have a wonderful home. She would have attention and love lavished on her like never before, and she wouldn't have to put up with Veronica's mood swings.

After standing patiently for half an hour while everyone talked, Garnet stuck her nose out all of a sudden and neighed loudly. Laughing, Katie took the reins over her head. "Come on, girl, I'll put you away now." Of course The Saddle Club wouldn't hear of letting Katie untack by herself, so they all trooped back to the stall together.

As soon as they had Garnet cross tied and Mrs. Miller had gone off to the office to telephone Dr. Weicker, Max appeared, as if on cue. Everyone tried to explain all at once and pretty soon Max gathered that Garnet was sold. He introduced himself to Mr. Miller, and the two men chatted politely.

"I have to confess, I'm not as surprised as I should be," Max said. "I was passing the ring an hour ago, and I happened to look in and see somebody jumping Garnet in excellent form. So I was hoping things would work out this way."

Katie turned bright red at Max's praise and mumbled a thank-you.

"Don't thank me. I'm just thrilled that Garnet is going to have a new owner," Max said. "I mean, the *right* new owner," he added hastily.

The Saddle Club grinned: That was about as close a slip as Max had ever made concerning Veronica. It was a moment to savor.

"Everything's all set. Dr. Weicker will be here tomorrow morning," Mrs. Miller announced, rejoining the group.

"Yippee! Then I can have Garnet this week!" Katie cried.

Once Mrs. Miller had been introduced to Max, the three adults got down to business. The Millers wanted to pick Garnet up on Saturday as long as they could hire a trailer. They were going to assume that Garnet would vet out.

Meanwhile, Carole, Lisa, and Stevie started to tell Katie everything they knew about Garnet: about her quirks and habits, feeding and worming schedules, horse show experience, breeding. Katie listened with rapt attention. Then she told them about her plans to go for her next Pony Club rating in the spring and to try endurance trail riding, as she had mentioned before. She thanked The Saddle Club several times for calling her again.

"I guess you couldn't have known that even though Patch was a little too quiet, I'd want to ride Garnet again," Katie commented.

"It's funny how things work out sometimes," Stevie said with the utmost restraint.

Katie agreed. "You know, I have just one question about Garnet," she said. "No—two questions, I guess. One, none of you owns Garnet, and Max doesn't own her, so who does? And two, where is he? Or she?"

Stevie smiled. "Let me put it this way: It's a long story."

IT WAS HARD to believe that Garnet was sold. But the Millers had left a check with Max for the mare's full purchase price. Provided the vet gave her approval, Garnet had a new home.

When the Millers had driven away, Max congratulated Stevie, Lisa, and Carole on their first sale. "They're nice people, and the girl knows how to ride," he said, which, for Max, was very high praise. Then he raised one eyebrow. "I have just one question—no, *two* questions: One, I never did ask what was that emergency the Kingsleys' vet had to deal with, and two, were you planning to sell my best lesson horse?"

"It's a long story," The Saddle Club said in unison.

Surprisingly, Max accepted their answer with barely another raise of the eyebrow. He said he would call the diAngelos to tell them the good news, and went to start the evening feeding.

"Did I hear the Millers say that they wanted to have Garnet picked up on Saturday?" Stevie asked.

Carole nodded. "I think so."

"Good, that's perfect. It gives us time for the other thing I want to do," Stevie said mysteriously.

"What's that?" Lisa inquired.

"Let me put it this way: I have just one secret." She glanced at Carole. "No, actually two secrets. I'll let you guys in on one of them."

12

AFTER THE HORSE Wise Pony Club meeting on Saturday, Pine Hollow was abuzz with excitement. The horses were put away in a hurry. Then all the Pony Clubbers started pulling snacks and drinks out of their cubbies. The older kids, including Carole and Lisa, set up folding tables in the indoor ring. People darted back and forth bringing cups and napkins as well as carrots, apples, and sugar cubes.

Stevie stood in the middle of the hubbub with a satisfied smile on her face: She had organized so many parties at Pine Hollow that she wasn't even nervous about this one. Everybody had been eager to help out.

"Here comes the guest of honor now," Lisa said, pointing.

"Oh, good," Stevie said. "I was getting worried that she'd be late for her own going-away party."

"Garnet? Please," Carole said. "She's always been a lady."

As Betsy Cavanaugh led Garnet into the ring, Lisa stepped forward and snapped a few pictures. The chestnut mare looked wonderful. The Saddle Club had given her another extraspecial grooming, and, as an added touch, Lisa had braided red and yellow yarn into her mane. She entered the ring, raised her noble Arabian head, and then snorted loudly.

"Well, we're glad to see you, too," Carole kidded, giving Garnet a big pat.

As planned, Lisa said a few words of praise in honor of Garnet. "And even though we know she's going to have a great home at the Millers', we'll all miss her very much," she concluded. Everyone clapped and gathered around with their treats of carrots, apples, and sugar cubes. "I think we'd better hold off," Carole reminded them after Garnet had eaten a few. "She vetted out perfectly—we don't want her to show up at Katie's with colic!"

"Then we at least want Garnet's new owner to take the treats with her for future use," Polly Giacomin urged.

"I'm sure she'll be happy to," said Carole.

"Are we too late?" The party crowd turned in unison to see Max and Deborah hurrying in.

"Not if that's a cake!" Stevie cried.

Max and Deborah presented their offering to Garnet first. It was a big cake they'd bought at the grocery store, and it said "Bon Voyage!" Once Max was satisfied that Garnet had gotten a good look at it, he set it down and cut slices for everyone. Mrs. Reg had come, too. She poured hot cider from a huge thermos. Everyone took turns eating cake and holding Garnet.

In the middle of the party, a hush suddenly fell over the crowd. One look at the door to the ring revealed why: Veronica had finally shown up. Stevie had told Veronica about the plan, naturally—Garnet was her horse, after all —but she hadn't known whether Veronica would bother to come. Now that she had arrived, it was awkward. The Saddle Club had done so much work over the past couple of weeks to sell Garnet that it almost seemed as if she were their horse. Veronica seemed to recognize that. She came in quietly and greeted everyone. "I just got off the phone with the Kingsleys," she confided to the girls.

"Were they upset about Garnet?" Carole asked, feeling she had to, to be polite.

"Actually, no. It turns out Henrietta had decided to take

up waterskiing instead of riding. Who knows? They may have never sent their vet up." With that, Veronica seemed to have run out of things to say. She got herself a piece of cake and, looking almost embarrassed, went to stand with Garnet. When Stevie and Lisa looked over a few minutes later, Veronica had an arm on Garnet's neck and was talking softly to her.

"She's certainly behaving herself today," Lisa commented.

"Yeah, they both are: Garnet and Veronica," Stevie joked. "Imagine that."

Carole had retreated across the ring so that she could be alone and think. She noticed her friends laughing with each other. She wanted to join in, but she was having a hard time getting into the festivities. Every night that week she had talked to Cam, but he had been too busy packing to come see her or to have her come see him. Besides, his parents were too busy to drive him anywhere.

The whole thing had become final faster than Carole could have believed. Duffy was already on his way to California in a horse transport van; Cam would leave tomorrow. His parents had hired someone to drive their car across country so that the whole family could fly out to L.A. together. Several times Cam had promised that he would write, but Carole knew that even if he did, things would never be the same between them. They still didn't know each other all that well. Now they never would.

Lost in her brooding, Carole leaned back against one of the jumps and closed her eyes. She hardly knew how long she'd been there when she felt a hand tap her lightly on the shoulder. "Hey, sleepyhead. Worn out from all the horse selling?" a voice behind her asked.

Carole spun around. It was Cam! He looked happy to see her and pleased with his surprise presence at the party. "You came!" Carole cried.

Cam nodded. "Yup. Stevie invited me—I guess she wanted to keep it a secret. My mom had a few last-minute errands in Willow Creek anyway, so she dropped me off for a little while."

"I can't believe it!" Carole said. "I mean, I can't believe that you—or, Stevie—oh, never mind! You're really here!" She was so thrilled at seeing Cam one last time that she couldn't seem to say anything normal.

"I'm really here, and I really wanted to come," Cam assured her.

"Really?" Carole asked.

"Really," said Cam. He cleared his throat. "I wanted to come so I could give you this."

Carole felt her jaw drop as Cam reached into his pocket and held out a small box wrapped in paper with horses on it. "I have something for you, too. I was going to mail it, but now I can give it to you in person. Come on, it's in my cubby."

Carole noticed that Cam looked shyly pleased. Obviously he was glad that she had thought of him, too. Without further ado, she led him out of the ring and into the changing room. She fished around in her cubby and brought it out. She hadn't had time to wrap it, so she made Cam close his eyes and stick out his hand. Then she placed her gift in his palm. It was a Saddle Club pin—the kind that Phil and A.J., as honorary Saddle Club members, already had. Carole had talked the gift idea over with Lisa and Stevie, and they had agreed that Cam definitely deserved to be an out-of-town Saddle Club member. He more than met the requirements: He was horse-crazy, and he'd always been a good friend.

"Okay, open your eyes," Carole said.

Cam opened his eyes. His expression changed from curious to delighted. "It's a Saddle Club pin, isn't it?" he asked.

Carole nodded shyly. "Stevie and Lisa and I all wanted you to have it."

Cam pinned it to his jacket immediately. "I can't wait till somebody at the Los Angeles Equestrian Center asks me where I got this," he said. "I'll tell them, 'Sorry, but it's a very exclusive club,'" Cam joked. "All right, now you open yours."

Carole fumbled with the wrapping paper on her box but finally got it open. "You got me a pin, too!" she exclaimed.

"I guess great minds think alike," said Cam, smiling.

Inside the box was a horseshoe-shaped stickpin. Carole could hardly believe Cam had picked out such a perfect gift. She gulped a little before she managed a thank-you.

"When I saw it, it reminded me of the good-luck horse-shoe here that you told me about," Cam said. "I . . ." He hesitated and looked down, shoving his hands into his pockets. "I'll still be a good friend, you know, Carole. At least, I'll try to be."

Carole could read more from Cam's face than from what he said. He seemed to realize, like her, how hard long-distance friendships could be, especially when the friend-ship was just getting started. All of a sudden Carole was conscious of the silence. She wanted to break it, but, for the millionth time, she didn't know what to say. "Cam . . ."

"Yes?"

Carole paused a minute as the door to the changing room swung open. Veronica strode in, her cheeks wet with tears. She stopped in her tracks when she saw Cam and Carole. "Oh . . . hi. I didn't know anyone was in here." Abruptly Veronica wiped her face with her hand. "There's so much dust in the barn, I must have gotten some in my eyes," she said, visibly trying to compose herself.

"Is the party still going on?" Carole asked, tactfully changing the subject.

Veronica shook her head. "It's just about over. Katie's here for Garnet now."

"Wow, we'd better go see her off," Carole realized.

"Yeah, she'll be gone soon," Veronica added, almost wistfully.

"I'm going to miss that horse," said Carole, hoping to put Veronica at ease. "She's a sweetheart."

"Yes, she is sweet . . ." Veronica's voice trailed off. Then she seemed to snap back to attention. "She's awfully sweet—but then there's Danny. You wouldn't exactly call him 'sweet,' but he's still the perfect horse. Everyone agrees. Even Max can't fault him. Did you know—"

By silent, mutual consent, Cam and Carole headed for the door, nodding and smiling. They weren't about to get trapped listening to Veronica bragging while Garnet left for her new home.

Outside, Stevie and Lisa were helping Katie put up the

ramp of the trailer. All the kids had gathered to say their final good-byes. Once the ramp was secure, Katie hugged each of The Saddle Club members in turn, ending with Carole, who ran up to join the group. Then Katie picked up the basket of treats the Pony Clubbers had given Garnet and hopped into the front seat of the truck. She rolled the window down and waved. "Maybe we'll see you at Pony Club events!"

"Don't forget to write!" Lisa called. She had made Katie promise to keep them posted on Garnet's progress as an endurance trail horse.

"And that goes for you, too, Garnet!" Stevie called. "No excuses!"

"Bye, everyone!" Katie called.

The group waved and called their good-byes. Stevie, Lisa, and Carole stood together and watched the trailer as it lumbered down the driveway. Finally it rounded the corner and the chestnut rump disappeared from view. The three girls sighed. It was hard to watch an old friend leave, human or equine. Carole was so preoccupied with watching Garnet go off to her new home that she momentarily forgot that her time with Cam was almost over. But while the trailer had pulled out, another car had pulled in. All at once Carole realized that it was Cam's mother in her station wagon. Stunned that Mrs. Nelson had arrived so quickly, she turned to look for Cam. She didn't have to look far: He was right beside her. Before she could think of what to say, he leaned down. Right in front of everyone, he gave her a kiss—so quick she hardly felt it—and then he was gone, too.

ON SUNDAY MORNING Carole woke up feeling tired. She hit the Snooze button on her alarm twice before she got out of bed. Normally she leaped out of bed on the weekends, knowing that she had a whole day to spend at Pine Hollow. But this morning she felt depressed. She was depressed about Cam's moving, and she was even a little depressed about Garnet's leaving. The Saddle Club had worked so hard to find the perfect new owner for the mare that Carole felt she had really gotten to understand her. Before the past couple of weeks, Garnet had always been Veronica's domain, so Carole hadn't been able to get to know her as much as, say, Prancer or Belle. And now both Cam and Garnet had left just when she was liking them most.

Carole knew she couldn't sit around and mope all day. What she needed was a good long trail ride on Starlight— and she hadn't had one all week! She picked up the phone beside her bed and used three-way calling to dial Lisa and Stevie. The two of them said they couldn't think of a better way to spend the morning.

Carole got dressed in a hurry, splashed water on her face, and went downstairs, where Colonel Hanson insisted on feeding her a huge breakfast of scrambled eggs, hash browns, and sausage. Carole knew he was trying to cheer her up after yesterday, and the food did taste good. On the drive over to Pine Hollow, she thanked her father for being so nice.

"Hey, you're not the only one who's going to miss Cam," Colonel Hanson said. "I was getting used to our phone conversations, you know."

WITHIN AN HOUR Carole, Lisa, and Stevie were in the saddle and headed for the woods. The twin departures were on everyone's mind. "All I can think is how glad I am that it was Katie disappearing down the road with Garnet and not any of the other prospective buyers," Stevie said.

132

"But darling Henrietta was so wonderful after six weeks, imagine her in six years!" Lisa said.

"*She's* nothing that a crop and spurs wouldn't cure!" said Carole.

"And what about Rose Marie Ambrosia Lee? She just wanted a nice little ole Arab for herself. Don't you think Garnet would have looked cute as Scarlett O'Hara's horse?" Lisa teased.

"Yeah—if Rose Marie Ambrosia Lee looked anything like Scarlett O'Hara," Stevie said.

"Seriously, though," Carole said, "it was a pretty good Saddle Club project, all in all, when you think about where Garnet might have ended up."

"I wish we hadn't had to do the project at all," Lisa said. "If Veronica was as concerned as she should have been about Garnet, she would have made sure Garnet found a good home. We wouldn't have had anything to do. She just never cared about Garnet."

"Actually, I think she must have cared a little," Carole said. She told them how she was sure she had seen Veronica crying when Garnet left. At first they wouldn't believe her, but then Stevie came up with a theory to explain Veronica's sudden change of heart.

"At least Garnet always responded to any affection that Veronica gave her. Now that Veronica's trying hard to take good care of Danny, the horse is ignoring her completely. Maybe Veronica didn't realize how special Garnet was until it was too late," she mused.

At that moment a cardinal flew up from a bush beside the trail. Carole watched it soar into the air. "Cam's plane must be up there somewhere—they had an early flight out of D.C. this morning," she said.

Stevie and Lisa offered a few words of comfort—Cam might write; Carole might be on the West Coast sometime—but they knew that there wasn't much they could do. Carole would miss Cam no matter what.

"Hey, look at that log up ahead." Lisa pointed at a fallen tree in their path. "It's the perfect size. Let's jump it."

The girls shortened their reins. Stevie led off, followed by Lisa and then Carole. Keeping a safe distance behind her friends, Carole cantered toward the jump. The cool winter air stung her face. They were two strides—then one stride away. Then Starlight soared, and Carole's heart, despite everything, lifted with joy.

ABOUT THE AUTHOR

BONNIE BRYANT is the author of more than a hundred books about horses, including The Saddle Club series, Saddle Club Super Editions, the Pony Tails series, and Pine Hollow, which follows the Saddle Club girls into their teens. She has also written novels and movie novelizations under her married name, B. B. Hiller.

Ms. Bryant began writing The Saddle Club in 1986. Although she had done some riding before that, she intensified her studies then and found herself learning right along with her characters Stevie, Carole, and Lisa. She claims that they are all much better riders than she is.

Ms. Bryant was born and raised in New York City. She still lives there, in Greenwich Village, with her two sons.